CROSSING THE LINE

A Tale of Two Teens in the Gaza Strip

by Alexandra Powe Allred

Perfection Learning®

Cover Illustration: Michael A. Aspengren

Dedication

This book was especially difficult to write because of the complicated nature of the subject. It would not have been possible without the advice, encouragement, and expertise of those who have read and contributed to *Crossing the Line*. A profound thank-you to: **Phyllis Blaunstein**, Senior Consultant of the Widmeyer Group; **Mike Center**, CEO of Operational Software Security Solutions, Inc. and expert in Middle Eastern affairs; **Marc Powe**, Deputy Director of African Affairs—Office of the Secretary of Defense, and former Defense Attaché of the Middle East; **Wajahat Sayeed**, CEO of the Muslim Legal Fund; and **Rashidah Id Deen**, Crisis Counselor/Author.

For information, contact
Perfection Learning® Corporation
1000 North Second Avenue, P.O. Box 500
Logan, Iowa 51546-0500.
Phone: 1-800-831-4190
Fax: 1-800-543-2745
perfectionlearning.com

PB ISBN-13: 978-0-7891-6017-1 ISBN-10: 0-7891-6017-x
RLB ISBN-13: 978-0-7569-1370-0 ISBN-10: 0-7569-1370-5

3 4 5 6 7 8 PP 12 11 10 09 08 07

About the Author

Alexandra Powe Allred has a B.A. from Texas A&M University, where she majored in history and minored in Russian. As the daughter of a U.S. diplomat, Allred spent many years overseas, in Russia, Tunisia, Iraq, and Germany.

In 1994, she was named Athlete of the Year by the U.S. Olympic Committee and won a gold medal at the U.S. Nationals in women's bobsledding.

She is the author of several sports books including *The Quiet Storm* and *Atta Girl!* In addition she has written *Atticus Weaver and His Triumphant Leap from Outcast to Hero and Back Again*, *The Code*, *Entering the Mother Zone*, *Passion Rules! Inspiring Women in Business*, and a dog obedience book.

Currently, Allred maintains her passion for sports as a professional football player for the WPFL's Austin Rage. She is raising three young children with her husband, Robb.

Table of Contents

Preface

Many of us have watched scenes on the nightly news showing fighting among people from a faraway place. We soon understand that this is what seems to be an endless conflict between two groups of people trying to share the same small country. We see youths throwing rocks, soldiers shooting back, and a constant refrain that each side is retaliating for what the other did yesterday or last month or 50 years ago.

The place is Israel, and the issue is how people called Palestinians will share the land of Israel with, of course, the Israelis. But *why* is that so hard to solve? What are Occupied Territories? The West Bank of what? And what in the world is the Gaza Strip? And *why* are they fighting, and *how* will the conflict ever be resolved?

Those of us who pay a bit more attention understand that the Palestinians are Arabs who were conquered by the Israelis more than 50 years ago when the Israelis created a new country called Israel. But *why* would that still be a problem? Well, we can soon learn that most (but not all) Israelis are Jews, and many of them were survivors of the persecution of Jews in Europe called the Holocaust during World War II. They returned to what they considered to be a land given to them by God.

Ok, so what's the issue? The issue is that the Palestinians are Arabs, most (but not all) of whom are Muslims and who already lived in this same small area. When the Jews said they wanted to establish their own country, neighboring Arab

Preface

countries tried and failed to defeat the Jews. Israel was born, and so was a long conflict over the land.

All of this is far from the United States, and for most Americans it is a conflict that is easier to ignore than to try to understand. Even when something called the Intifada led to violent conflict, this was still not our problem.

Everything changed on the morning of September 11, 2001. Now we have to recognize that we are all connected, and what happens to one group of people on the other side of world does—and should—have meaning to all of us. In this case, the anger that one group of people felt carried across the world and brought vast destruction and terror to the United States.

My own children began asking me questions that were very complicated, and I must confess that I had a hard time answering them. What they were learning from people around us was that Muslims or Arabs or Middle Easterners are bad. I knew that was wrong, but I needed both facts *and* a way to explain them to my children. I spoke with analysts and professors of Middle East studies; experts from the United Nations, the Pentagon, and security agencies; as well as members of the Jewish, Muslim, and Christian faiths.

I concluded that the best way to help children understand the tremendously complicated issues involved would be to use fictional characters set in the actual situation. While the names of the places used in the book are real as is much of the dialogue (taken straight from news headlines and stories), the tale of Binyamin and Ahmet is fictionalized.

Preface

These characters speak in their own voices, expressing the biases they have against their perceived enemies. Some of the angry remarks will be offensive to readers, but I believe that hearing the anger is essential to understanding *why* they hate, *why* they fight, and *why* this conflict is so hard to resolve. The fact that some of my reviewers thought the book was too critical of one side, and others thought it was unbalanced in the other direction, encourages me to believe I have succeeded in some small measure in conveying both the Israeli and the Palestinian viewpoints. My fondest hope is that this story will help children (and adults) answer their most common questions.

Without question, I have over-simplified the Palestinian crisis. For example, I have not tried to explain that there are Israeli Arabs and there are Christian Palestinians. Instead, I chose to let the story put the issue in the most basic terms: a contest of force between Muslims and Jews over one land.

If the book succeeds, readers will come away from it with a greater understanding of what is happening in the Middle East and a stronger concern about the terrible events that so terrorize people there. This can lead to an understanding that if we are tolerant of one another's legitimate beliefs and work together, we can change the world—for the better. Education is the key: The more we understand one another, the better we can communicate, and that is what Binyamin and Ahmet are trying to do.

1

Ahmy

RUNNING

THE knock came late at night. It was so urgent and so loud, Ahmy knew what it was. War had broken out. Again. For days he had sensed how tense everyone had become. Men stood in the streets shouting at one another. But it wasn't just happening here, Ahmy knew. It was happening all along the Gaza Strip. Food had become increasingly scarce as battles broke out along the outer towns in the West Bank. It was as though they lived on a giant chain. Each Palestinian village that got sucked into various battles broke the chain that delivered food, medical aid, and communication from the outside world. And Ahmet Aziz, or Ahmy as his family called him, knew that to stay in this village about to be swallowed whole by war was suicide. Mortar shells would bomb the buildings, thinking nothing of small children and babies.

"Ahmy," he heard his mother call to him in the darkness. "Ahmy, take Madi's hand!" Like Ahmy, his young brother Mohibullah was called a familiar pet name by his loved ones. Madi was only three years old and far too little to understand what was going on. He was too little to know how scared he should really be. He was too little to know that Ahmy once had another brother. But that brother had been killed by the Jews. "Take his hand, and do not lose him," his mother instructed.

In the dark, Ahmy nodded, desperately groping for his sandals on the cool concrete floor. Across the room, someone had opened the front door.

"They are coming!" a man said. "There is no time for anything but to run."

"Ahmy! Ahmy!" his mother called again, this time more loudly.

"There is no place left for us to go!" Ahmy suddenly heard his father shouting. "The tanks roll through our homes as though they mean nothing, as though we mean nothing!"

"Abdel!" Ahmy's mother muttered under her breath. She shot a look at Ahmy. "This does not help us now," she whispered harshly. "Words do not help us now." Ahmy's mother was frantically running about trying to get clothes and food together. She was trying to get Summi, his baby sister, swaddled up for another long and certainly dangerous journey. Ahmy's father was no help. Fury had consumed him, and he seemed oblivious to what was going on around him.

Ahmy's fingertips had just touched the side of one of his sandals when the blast sent everyone forward. Both Summi and Madi began crying, and Ahmy's mother screamed. A bomb had hit a house not too far from where they all sat or stood. The enemy was moving in rapidly, and Ahmy knew they thought nothing of killing babies.

"Dear God! Where are we to go?" Ahmy's father roared over the sounds of panic. Outside, others were screaming and running. Ahmy forgot his sandals and scrambled to his feet, fighting to find Madi in the darkness, take his hand, and flee. Any moment, their small house would be bombed. Tables, chairs, and pottery would all be blown to bits. Rocks and walls would crumble like dry sand, and praise be to God if no humans were nearby when the violence struck. If they were lucky.

"What is happening?" Madi asked, but Ahmy could afford no time for explanations. It was all so horrible and confusing, and it had been happening for so long. How could he explain it to Madi? Now or anytime? He could hardly understand it himself. Palestinians and Jews were fighting over a piece of land. Both sides claimed the land belonged to them. Ahmy knew whose land it really was. But this did not matter to the Israelis.

"Abdel! Help your family! They are coming!" Ahmy's mother screamed. Now standing, Ahmy could see out the opened front door. He saw shadows of frightened villagers fleeing into the night. He could tell by the glow in the darkness and the smell that a fire was burning. Somewhere a house was on fire, and briefly he hoped no one was trapped inside. He had seen that too. He had seen what it looked like after a home had been burned.

"Who? Who is coming?" Madi wanted to know as Ahmy grabbed his little hand and pulled him close. Ahmy was preparing himself for the door, for the open run. They were coming, but he would have to survive the run as well. He could hear the sounds of panicked people— once neighbors and friends. But now the people were running for their lives, and they would just as easily trample him to death as scream.

Another blast ripped through the town, causing the earth and buildings around them to shake.

"This is not how a man should live!" screamed Abdel, punching his clenched fist at the ceiling. "How can this be?!" But his wife only pushed him aside and screamed for Ahmy. Hiba Aziz, too, had lived through this many times, and

she was not going to stand still while the enemy
fire drew closer. She paused at the door frame,
clutching her baby in her arms, waiting for the
right time to step into the narrow street and run
with the others. Like everyone else, she had
heard that a new United Nations settlement had
been established inside the border of Jordan. It
was the safest place to run, if they could just get
there.

Madi's eyes were huge as he watched his
older brother. He was just too little to
remember he had been through this before.
"Who is coming, Brother?" he asked Ahmy. His
voice was strangely calm, and it caught Ahmy off
guard for just a moment. In the midst of
complete terror and madness, Madi needed to
know who he should be frightened of.

"The Jews, little one. The Israelis are
coming."

Then over his shoulder, Ahmy heard his
father's grave voice. "Again. They come again.
And they will keep coming until they have every
last piece of land and property and dignity from
us . . . But for now, there is nothing we can do
but run."

With a slight nudge, Abdel pushed Ahmy
and Madi out of the house and into the stream
of frightened people running for shelter.

1

Binny

RUNNING

BINNY checked over his shoulder again. Something was out there. He could sense it. At first, he had thought it was his imagination. Since the death of those Palestinian boys, everyone was jumpy. The Palestinians were claiming that the Israelis had had something to do with it. But that was so typical of them. In truth, as Binny's father had explained it, those Muslim boys had been up to no good. They had been concocting a bomb of their own. It was the way of the Muslims. Instead of bettering their land or their homes, they gathered in little mobs to make more plans of war and destruction.

Palestinian leaders had made other claims. They said the boys had been on their way to school when they had stepped on a land mine planted by the Israeli soldiers. Binny knew different. Those boys never went to school. Always, they were trying to throw homemade bombs and fire rocks from slingshots into Binny's compound, and they didn't care who they hit.

Binyamin Peres lived in Kfar Darom, a Jewish settlement in the Gaza Strip. It was just one of many well-organized Israeli settlements for residents in the West Bank and Gaza. It was something that made Binny proud. His people had fought hard for the land and worked even harder to raise crops and become a self-sufficient people. Personally, this was where he liked to spend most of his time. When he was not in school, he liked to be outside working the crops. For a moment, he could forget about the war that raged back and forth between the two communities—Muslims and Jews. Palestinians and Israelis. They were so close in proximity, yet so far from each other. The way they saw life, religion, and family were completely different.

There it was again. Binny stiffened. He had been lost in thought for a moment. With the early morning sun beating down on his back, he felt warmed and alone. Now he felt his pulse quicken. *Alone.* This was not a good place to be alone.

Although the settlement was fiercely protected by Israeli soldiers, Muslim militants could find a way to sneak in or lob some dangerous weapon over the wall that was built around Kfar Darom. They were never at work.

They were never doing anything constructive or beneficial to their own communities! Always, they were lurking about the confines of Kfar Darom, waiting to find an innocent Jew alone to attack. And here he sat pruning tomato plants—the perfect target.

He turned his head sideways, hoping to catch a glimpse of someone or a movement. He did not want to give himself away by showing that he had heard the intruder. Slowly, Binny turned his head, pretending to rub his nose against his shoulder, and glanced up. Nothing. The rising sun peeked over the wall to Kfar Darom, making it difficult for Binny to see anything in that direction. He looked again, moving dirt around and appearing to be busy with his work. Instead, he listened to everything—the wind, his own breathing, birds, the sounds of the villagers off in the distance working and moving about. It was life as usual for everyone else.

He heard it again. A shuffle. That unmistakable sound of pebbles scuffing against the sole of one's shoe. Then silence.

Slowly, Binny turned. The constant threat of the young Palestinians was unbearable at times. Kfar Darom was his home. By birthright! Again and again, he had learned in his lessons, heard from his father, and read in the Torah, that this was the land of the chosen people—*his* people. Binny had every right to be here, and he had learned to love this land. Unlike whatever renegade lurked outside the wall like some coward, Binny actually worked the land. He studied and worked and prayed. This was his home and his land.

There was a time when the land had belonged to the Palestinians, but long before that, the land had been designated for the "chosen people." Clearly, it was the destiny of his people that they would always have to fight for what was theirs and what was right. Binny stood fully, facing whoever was hiding in the shadows.

He thought about speaking out. He thought about calling to some of the men in Kfar Darom he knew to be armed and ready to fight. But before he could make a decision, he was hit. The force was brutal, and it nearly knocked the wind out of him. The rock fell hard against his shoulder, rocking him back and nearly knocking him from his feet. As he stumbled, he heard the heavy thuds of other stones around him. He was under siege!

A cheer came from atop the wall, and he could dimly see the figures of three boys. Binny winced. Holding his shoulder with a free hand, he squinted against the sun, afraid to turn his back and run and wanting desperately to see the faces of his assailants. He wanted them to see that he was not afraid.

Another hit. This time against his thigh, and he let out a yell that was quickly followed by a victory whoop from the other side. The pain was overwhelming. It felt as if something had struck right against his bone. The Palestinians had become so proficient at their stone throwing and slingshots, the stones were nearly as dangerous as any bullet. Binny knew the Muslims were toying with him. They could have struck him in the head had they really wanted. Binny was struck a third time, this time in the shin bone, and it was a shot so painful, it brought him to his knees.

More than ever, Binny wanted to call out for help. More than ever, he was determined to remain quiet. He would not give his assailants that satisfaction. He would not let them hear fear. He struggled to his feet again and stared hard against the sun. Even the brightness felt like it was burning holes into his eye sockets. Shadows. Dark shadows was all he could see. But they were young. No older than Binny himself. He could see from the outline of their bodies they were not quite men—teenage boys. Three in all.

Binny drew in his breath as he saw one step away from the others, lift his slingshot high, and draw back an elbow. The Palestinian held that position for a moment, angling in on Binny. Binny took a step backward. Then another. He could hear them laughing at him, taunting him, yelling that he was running to his mother and father. Binny could feel his face grow hot. It was true—he was embarrassed by the name-calling, but more than that, he was furious. Everyone present knew that he could be dead in the blink of an eye. His attacker held the stone, ready to strike, but waited.

"You should go back to where you came from," the voice called to Binny. "This is not your home! This is our home!"

No one moved.

This was so typical of how they acted, Binny thought. He had been minding his own business, tending to the family garden, when they attacked him. On his soil. In his home. And they tell to him to leave! Then the one holding the slingshot made a fake movement with his elbow, as though he were going to release the rock. Binny turned and ran.

"See him run!" the voices called after him. "See how he runs . . . Jews are all cowards."

2

Ahmy

OUR LAND

How could he tell a three-year-old how
their land had been taken from them and how
the Jews terrorized the Muslims because of
their faith? How could he tell his little brother
that they once had a brother who died because
of the Israelis? How could Madi understand
how their own people were forced to live in the
very worst conditions? Madi could not
understand it. Not now. But there would come
a time when he did, and he would be very angry
about the loss of his brother and his land. He
would be so furious over the way his people had
been forced to live that it would consume his
every thought, and he would think of nothing
else but revenge. It wasn't right. Ahmy knew
this. But it was how *he* felt.

"Once," he explained to Madi, "Father
was a very successful merchant. We were quite
prosperous and enjoyed a good life. Clothing,
food, and education." He waved a hand,
showing Madi how much they'd had. "We had
many nice things, Madi."

It wasn't something Ahmy usually talked about, much less thought about. It was so long ago. But as he spoke to his little brother, the memories flooded in. He had been born and raised in the Jordanian-controlled West Bank of Palestine. He could remember their home with plush carpeting, stuffed pillows, and beautiful pottery that his mother had collected and placed about the house. Fruits, nuts, and cakes were plentiful. He could remember how he would lie on his back in his small but cozy room, stare up at the ceiling when he was supposed to be napping, and listen to the sounds from the market. A warm breeze always flowed through his room, causing the sheer linen curtains to dance and twirl above his head. As merchants and customers bartered over the price of foods and goods, it began almost a melodic hum that eased him to sleep. Sleep had always been so sweet. He could remember that well.

"But that changed the night a horrible battle erupted between Israel, Jordan, Egypt, and Syria. Father says many people died. Soldiers fired upon one another with renewed hatred." Ahmy looked down at his little brother. Madi's eyes were huge. Just how much he could understand, Ahmy did not know. Still, he talked on. It was as much for Madi as it was for himself. He reassured himself as they walked through the night. "The soldiers fought over little pieces of land, about who should be here and who should be there. No one could ever be happy where they were.

"This is a funny thing, Madi, because I was happy. Father and Mother were happy. Then the pounding came to our door. I remember how Mother had been shushing everyone, but it was too late. We were all awake. And I could hear her prayers." Ahmy shook his head at this. He could still hear her voice in his head, so he shook his head a little harder, hoping to knock it out. She had been so frightened. He had heard the fear in her voice as she asked God for help and guidance.

"But the Israeli soldiers cared nothing for her pleas," Ahmy continued. "They told us to leave at once . . . or we would be killed." None of this meant anything to Madi, he knew. Madi was too little to understand such things. Ahmy frowned. All of their rugs and pillows and pictures and pottery had been left behind. Clothes and food were forbidden. Ahmy and his family had been forced to walk through the night without shoes, still wearing their night clothing.

Of the actual trip, Ahmy could remember little. Perhaps, like Madi, he had been too young. But what happened as a result of that trip burned so sharply in Ahmy's mind, it could have easily happened the day before. The feelings he had because of that fateful journey were so raw and so real, he felt tortured all over again. Vaguely, he could remember that they had walked throughout the night and that he had cried, wanting to stop. His father had carried him while his mother carried his brother. He remembered that when they had stopped to rest, his mother's feet were bleeding. His father's feet bled too.

Just reliving that trip made Ahmy wet his lips. He remembered how thirsty he'd been. Those were his most vivid memories. No water. No food.

"We were all so weak. Father now says he thought we wouldn't make it to the refugee camp."

"Why?" Madi chirped, and Ahmy jumped a little. He had almost forgotten he was talking to Madi.

"He thought we would all die of starvation out in the middle of nowhere. But we did make it to the U.N. refugee camp. There were no bathrooms, and sand covered everything—including the food. But at least there *was* food—and water and shelter."

It should have been the beginning of better times. But the refugee camps had been crude, with tents built upon other tents. Ahmy could not run and play. There was no school, no room to move without stepping on another person's tent. There were too many terrified and homeless people living in too small an area.

"So it was no surprise to anyone when a sickness traveled through the camp." At that, Ahmy stopped. He bit his lip and looked down at Madi, who seemed clueless about Ahmy's story. It was just as well. Madi did not need to know about the sickness. Ahmy sighed softly.

The germs and bacteria were something that couldn't be contained. The water supply was so limited, it could only be used for drinking. There was little to no bathing or washing hands.

There had been a few U.N. and European doctors on hand, trying their best to help. But the cholera epidemic could not be stopped for weeks. The sickness had traveled fast and furiously through the tents, killing the elderly and the very young. Ahmy hadn't understood about germs and such things. He had been too young. But he learned all too quickly when he helped his father bury his little brother, when he sat with his mother as she cried until her throat was raw, and when he promised himself that he would have his own home again.

"It will be much better this time," he said to Madi, struggling to sound optimistic. It *had* to be better this time, Ahmy thought.

It was hard to know exactly where they were. As a baby and small child, Ahmy had crossed and recrossed the Jordan River many times. What did it matter anyway? It wasn't home. It did not matter where they ran. It would still never be home.

As the Aziz family picked their way through the refugee camp, Ahmy held Madi's hand. Each time Madi reached out to touch something or pick something up, as he loved to do, Ahmy jerked his hand. He knew he was being rough with Madi, but he was terrified of Madi catching the sickness. Already, Ahmy could see the camp filling up with people, and he feared losing his little brother. He looked over to his mother who still carried Summi in her arms. Little Summi was also at great risk.

But things were a little better this time. An area had been designated strictly for the toilets and showers. The food was a little better and water more plentiful. Still, Ahmy let Madi touch nothing. There was so much his little brother didn't know and so much more Ahmy never wanted him to know.

On the first night of their stay in the Jordanian refugee camp, while his mother put Madi and Summi to bed, Ahmy crept out toward the edge of the camp where a large campfire burned and men gathered to talk. As a boy, he could walk about freely, and no one questioned why he was out and about. It was his one blessing.

"We have to return," said one man. "Do you not see what is happening? Each day they take a little more, drive us back like cattle. Soon we will have nothing unless we return."

"Yes, return and fight," said another.

"Fight with what?" a third asked. "We have nothing. They have guns and weapons of all kinds. We have nothing."

There was much muttering, and several different conversations broke off among the men. Ahmy scooted up toward the fire, finding an empty, overturned gas can lying nearby. He sat on it, resting his elbows on his knees. No one seemed to even notice him.

"Quiet. Everyone, please. Listen to me." The man who spoke was the one who had suggested returning to their homeland to fight. As Ahmy watched him, he realized he had seen him before. He seemed to be someone the others looked to for guidance. He was not a large man. In fact, he was smaller than Ahmy's father, Abdel. But his voice was booming and his gaze so intense that Ahmy understood why the men listened to him. His name, Ahmy would later learn, was Mawlawi Azduk. Sitting before the warm fire under the open sky, Ahmy listened as Mawlawi Azduk retold the history of the Palestinian people over the last half-century.

"We should not forget the year 1948! It was the year that Israel defeated the Arabs who had been living in and governing the state of Palestine. So violent were these Jews and so swift was their brutality that the Arabs fled in fear. What else could they do? They were being slaughtered! But when these poor souls left, the Israelis established the state of Israel, forcing the Palestinians to turn to the Gaza Strip and West Bank. Our home was changed forever.

"This, then, was to be our safe haven," Mawlawi Azduk recounted to his audience. "This was where we would live and rebuild our lives!" The Gaza Strip was not a traditional part of the newly formed Israel, so many families settled there in refugee camps while others fled across the Jordan River to the West Bank.

"How did it come to be that we were forced to live in these refugee camps?" Mawlawi Azduk spread his arms wide and turned in a tiny circle, casting his gaze on each man and boy who could hear him speak. It was a startling question, and for a moment, Ahmy was lost in his own question: How could *they* be refugees in a land that was theirs and where *they* were in the majority? He looked around for a moment. Tents and squalor. Crying mothers, hungry babies. Sickness would be coming soon. His eyes shifted to his father. Abdel Aziz was sitting on the ground, oblivious to anything but the words of Mawlawi Azduk. Ahmy could see that his father's teeth and fists were clenched, and for the first time he understood his father's anger. And he had to wonder if Abdel Aziz thought of Ahmy's little brother—the baby they had had to bury somewhere in the desert.

Mawlawi Azduk's voice boomed.

"From 1948 to 1967, the Jews created and maintained the state of Israel from the southern border of Lebanon, including the Jordan River Valley, Sea of Galilee, and half of Jerusalem," he counted off on his fingers. "But it was not enough! Oh, no! In 1967, the Israelis made a lightning attack that captured all of Jerusalem, the West Bank, and the Golan Heights, making the state of Israel much larger and more powerful. Suddenly, they were governing cities where most of the residents were Arabs."

In 1973, there had been another bloody war—one that Ahmy had heard about many times. It had taken the lives of many of his uncles and great-uncles. Ahmy's father had been there. It was his turn to speak about how the Arabs had decided to fight for what was theirs. "Then early one morning," Abdel Aziz began, "we launched a new war in hopes of regaining our land. In numbers, we were strong! Especially the Egyptian Army that crossed the Suez Canal and drove the Israelis back. Many brave men had gone to fight!" But they were, as Ahmy's father explained, highly disconnected. Once on the battlefields, they had no way of talking to other fighting groups. Their weapon supply was low, and they resorted mostly to hand-to-hand combat and slingshots. Ultimately, surprise was not enough. They were no match for the well-armed Israeli soldiers. The United States and some European countries had embraced their Jewish brothers, damning the Arabs. As a result, the Jews had an endless sea of bullets and weapons.

"It was not meant to be," Mawlawi Azduk said rather dejectedly. For a moment, his shoulders slumped. Everyone watched him in silence. Only the crackling of the fire dared to make a noise as Mawlawi Azduk collected his thoughts. He appeared to study the sand for a moment. Ahmy imagined that even the sand would grow nervous under such a gaze. Slowly, Mawlawi Azduk shook his head. "As it is today, my brothers, we are fighting against something much bigger than the Israeli Army."

It was easy, sometimes, to get angry at the world. How, Ahmy wondered, could the rest of the world side with the Israelis when they were so clearly in the wrong? But it had only gotten worse. In the years that followed, the Israeli government began to expand their ownership of land, terrorizing the Palestinian refugees and creating more and more Jewish settlements like Kfar Darom.

"But our spirit cannot be denied!" proclaimed Mawlawi Azduk. "By God, *we* are the chosen people! This is our land . . . and no one should take that from us." He seemed to draw strength as more and more men echoed his sentiment. As fists were raised to the skies, Ahmy felt himself being swept away in the high emotions.

Again, Mawlawi Azduk stopped for a moment and gazed upon the fire that warmed him. He gathered his thoughts as his audience waited patiently. He was a man of great words. Waiting to hear them, Ahmy understood, was almost as good as hearing the actual words. Mawlawi Azduk stooped over and picked up the last piece of wood and threw it into the blaze. Out there, even their fire kindling had to be supplied by the United Nations. They were unable to care for themselves in all ways. The Israelis had taken away every bit of self-respect they could, and still they wanted more.

This last push from their homes had been too much for many, and this time the numbers would include Ahmy. He just wanted to have a home, go to school, and watch his little brother and sister grow up in peace, without the fear of the sickness killing them.

Sparks rose from the fire, and Mawlawi Azduk looked back to his audience. "This time, when they closed us out of our homes, they opened the door to destruction for themselves."

His voice was eerie. His eyes were coal-black as they danced with rage. There was a moment of silence and then loud whooping from the other men. There would be war. Again.

Binny

OUR LAND

"Do not dally," his mother called after him. Binny sighed. "I won't."

"You must always look around you. Never forget. Never be complacent," she warned, and Binny nodded his head. He knew the lecture well. Always, she said the same things over and over.

"I am always careful," he said and pulled the door quickly behind him. He was not annoyed with her. He knew she was just worried. There was much to be worried about. Kfar Darom was under renewed attack, and no one was safe.

Kfar Darom was a beautiful and mystical place for Binny and his family. In fact, this could be said of the entire Middle East. It was a land of ancient cities, vast deserts, and some of the oldest civilizations. And it was the birthplace of three of the most widespread religions in all the world—Judaism, Islam, and Christianity. It was an amazing place. It was a place where Binny believed he could feel his ancestors. It was a place that was blessed and celebrated by true believers. These narrow strips of fertile land on the densely populated Mediterranean coast made it a land of paradise. Most of the region was hot, dry, and barren, but there were also areas that were lush and bountiful. It was, or was certainly near, the center of the world!

"Binyamin!" His mother poked her head from the window and yelled down to him as he entered the street. He squinted up against the sky to see her. He could almost say her next words with her.

"Go only to the bakery and the merchant. Come straight home. No bus, no extra shops."

"Three places, Mother. The bakery, the merchant, and the gardens. Three places." He waved three fingers at her.

"And—" she started, but he finished for her. "Be careful!"

It was hard for Binny not to explore his surroundings. For all of his studies and readings, for all of his knowledge of the outside world, he had seen very little in his life. He stepped off the curb and headed into the market, but his mind wandered. Not too far from Kfar Darom was the Dome of the

Rock, a Muslim temple in Jerusalem. It was a site where the Muslim prophet Muhammad was believed to have ascended to heaven. The temple was said to house a rock that marked the center of the world. Near it was the Wailing Wall. Binny would have liked to visit the Dome of the Rock. But it was not a place welcome to Jews. However dangerous, he liked the idea that these two great religious sites were so close together. But no matter how close the two religious monuments were, the people of Israel and Palestine would never be close. He had heard of places where Palestinians and Israelis were actually neighbors yet never spoke a word to one another. For more than 30 years, some had never said a single word to their next-door neighbor.

Religion was a funny thing. Faiths, principles, and beliefs were based on religion. So, too, were wars. How could that be? Yet some of the bloodiest battles in history were over religion. The pyramids in Egypt had seen some bloody battles, but today people traveled from all over the world just to see the impressive structures. Binny had never seen the pyramids. Then again, he had never seen the Wailing Wall, and it was practically in his backyard.

He did not know how the Wailing Wall looked, but he imagined it would be something like Kfar Darom—a place busy with people who shared a common bond. It was busy inside the marketplace of Kfar Darom. A busy sort of energy ran through the square. People bartered for food and clothing. Peddlers called out for fair prices, and mothers hurried their children along, always rushing to one place or another. It had only been in the last year that Binny had been allowed to travel to the marketplace alone. He was a man in the family now, expected to run errands for his mother. He brought groceries and sewing supplies and carried messages back and forth among friends and family members across the compound for his mother and grandmother. To some, this would be menial work. But Binny loved it. He was outside and working for his family. And family, he had learned, was the most important thing in the world. Lately, his duties had expanded to working the family's plot of land in the community farm, repairing tools, and even bartering for new ones in the market square. It was an exciting time.

But it was also a frightening time. For as much as Binny loved the added responsibilities, he knew all of this was for another reason. Something was coming. Always, he had felt and embraced the energy in the market square, but he had felt an added urgency lately. A different kind of rushing and hurrying of his people. Mothers scurried small children in and out of shops quickly, wanting to get their chores done and be out of the marketplace as quickly as possible. A definite danger was brewing that could not be ignored.

Protected by armed soldiers, Kfar Darom was a kind of city to its own. It was a fortress, and Binny had always felt safe. The Israeli soldiers were tough. In fact, they were known around the world for their fierceness, their loyalty, and their training, but Binny knew the other side to these warriors. Most were very young men—18 and 19 years old. Most wanted to be shopkeepers, doctors, lawyers, or writers. But there was a mandatory draft in Israel, which meant that at 18, every boy became a man and a soldier, defending his land. And it wasn't just boys anymore. More and more female soldiers were protecting Kfar Darom as well. Perhaps because one day these young men and women would be living inside the settlement as civilians, raising families and beginning new businesses. Whatever their reason, their reputation as fierce warriors seemed strange to Binny. They weren't. They were just kids.

But a new wave of suicide bombers had changed things. There seemed to be a renewed anger among the Muslims that could not be quieted, and the Israeli soldiers were working harder than ever to keep things safe. The Palestinians assaulted the Israelis in every way imaginable, and then they cried foul when Binny's people retaliated. Could these people not see what they were doing? If the Palestinians would only leave them alone, everything would be all right. But the assaults and screaming and slingshots and threats continued. Not a day went by without more stories of settlers being attacked.

Although he had gone to the market for errands, Binny was also aware that the men of Kfar Darom had called a meeting. All the leaders from the different communities were coming together to discuss what should be done. It was a meeting that was closed to most of the public. However, there was a different meeting—one that everyone could attend. This was one that he had heard his neighbor call "the real meeting."

The real meeting?

"Our leaders," the man had laughed with a snort when Binny asked. "They won't do anything but talk. It's the men of our community—our fathers and sons, shopkeepers, merchants—who will make something happen. They are tired of being on the news everywhere in the world, depicted as living in a state of war rather than peace."

It was funny how even the most peaceful man—his neighbor, Jonathan Edelman—became agitated and animated when talking about religion.

"This is not what our religion is about!" Jonathan pounded one hand into the other. "We've come to Israel from Russia and Poland . . . My family is from England, you know. We've all come here not to make war, but rather, because we were called here!" His voice grew louder as he spoke. These were the same words Binny's own father spoke all the time. *We were the chosen people of this land. It was our destiny to be here, to create and support the state of Israel, to grow and prosper.* "These are not just my words," Jonathan went on, as though he read Binny's mind, "but those of our Jewish teachings. It is the word of God!"

As Binny entered the market, he could still hear the voice of his neighbor. *This is our home. Our home.* But the sounds of traffic, honking horns, shouts from peddlers, and busy shoppers gave Kfar Darom its own energy and life and soon drowned out everything else. Briefly, Binny paused to take it all in. This *was* home. He drew in a breath and turned to his right. The bakery. Then he stopped. To the left he saw a large group of men standing on a corner, just outside a grocery store, loudly debating.

The meeting.

Men were shouting at one another, cursing about the current state of affairs, and waving fists in the air.

"Instead of embracing Jews' rightful place and instead of embracing the fact that all the Middle East was the birthplace of so many different religions, the Arabs are trying to deny us our rightful place in history and geography!" shouted a young man. "It is an insult to us all!"

"But the violence," another protested. He was a young man, wearing wire-rimmed glasses with slightly unkempt hair and jeans. More than a dozen older men looked disapprovingly at him. This young man was part of a new movement among Kfar Darom's young people. Bright, educated, and thought to be radical in their ideas, they wanted peace among the Arab/Israeli world. And if that meant giving back some of the land to the Arabs, these young people were all for it.

"As a result of their violence, we are forced to fight back! And, yes, sometimes with brutality," the first man shouted back. Binny recognized him to be a merchant in the marketplace.

"This is not something we like to think about," said another man, directing his words toward the young man with glasses. "But what else can we do? Look at how the Palestinians behave. We cannot allow them to come here, into our home, and destroy us!"

"Perhaps," the young man said rather tentatively, "this is not entirely all our land." A loud grumble grew among those standing on the corner. Binny wiggled his way through the crowd, trying to edge closer to the center. The merchant's face grew dark as he shook his head at the young man.

"The massacre of Israelis at the 1972 Olympics was a clear example of that," the merchant retorted. "The only good that ever came from that horrific event was that all the world got to see just how terrible the Palestinians were. It was in their true nature to seek and destroy Jews—no questions asked!"

Binny loved sports, and he was especially fascinated with the Olympics. Perhaps that was why this story had always stuck with him, why he asked over and over again for the details. He kept pictures and newspaper clippings in a folder in his room. Without even looking at the pictures, he could see the masked men in his mind. So clearly. So horribly clearly, it was as if he had been there. Although not even born then, Binny knew all the morbid details.

In Munich, Germany, in 1972, a group of Palestinian terrorists from a group called Black September crept into the Olympic Village where athletes from all over the world slept and captured nine Israeli athletes.

The Palestinians wore black ski masks over their heads. They appeared on the balconies and in front of windows, holding guns and terrorizing the Israeli athletes. They claimed that they wanted the release of Palestinian prisoners, but they also wanted the world to see that their land was being taken away from them by the Israelis. To Binny's way of thinking, the Palestinians just wanted revenge against the Israelis. While they claimed to want sympathy from the world, they wore frightening ski masks, carried guns, and made threats. The Olympics and the world were paralyzed. No one knew how to act because Black September was very violent and might kill the athletes at any given moment. And when the German police moved in, trying to save the athletes, that was just what the Arabs did. They killed all the hostages.

Binny turned back to hear the men saying almost the same words. The Palestinians' protest at the Olympics did more harm than good to their own cause.

"You act as though this is a new problem," the merchant told the young man with glasses. With that, he gave a mock laugh. "Even before the 1972 Olympics, there was the 1947 war. But you are too young to know of this." He spat, and others around the man agreed. Then yet another man stepped forward. Binny was shoved back as the mouth of the circle in front of the shop opened even wider.

"The Arabs, the Palestinians, and now the Palestinian Liberation Organization, or PLO as they call themselves, have been determined for years to drive us out of our rightful land and reclaim, they say, what is theirs. They have been violent and brutal! They care nothing of killing women and children. They care nothing about tearing lives apart and destroying villages and homes. In 1947, the Arabs tried to crush the new Israeli nation and drive us into the sea."

"It was anti-Semitic," came a voice, and Binny recognized it at once. It was his father, Raanan Peres. "It was our Holocaust again! Ours is a land that God promised the Jews, and I intend to see that promise kept!"

A huge cheer erupted from the sidewalk. Binny tried to see the young man, to see what he was thinking or what he might say, but he was also pushed into the back of the crowd. Binny looked back to his father who was being congratulated. Heavy pats and hearty handshakes jostled his father's frame as he smiled back at everyone. Another young man gave Binny a sharp poke to the ribs and nodded approvingly, as though Binny might receive some of the credit for what his father had just said. Binny nodded back, then withdrew from the crowd. He still really wanted to hear what the young man with glasses might say.

Fighting his way backward, he reached the edge of the curb and felt fresh air. He stepped away from the large crowd and, for a moment, into the street so that he might see better. The young man was walking away, headed toward a local café very popular with the young adults.

"Uh," Binny called out hesitantly as he hustled after the man. "Hello! I . . . wanted to talk to you." The man turned and waited for Binny to catch up. "Uh, what you said back there . . ." He poked a thumb back toward the crowd.

The young man snorted. "They won't listen."

"I will," Binny answered.

"Look, I am not saying what the Palestinians are doing is right," the young man began. "It isn't. But the Palestinians believe that the land they call Palestine is theirs. As much as we say it's ours, they say it's theirs. Do you understand? All I am saying is, it's difficult to be angry with them at times because they think the same way we do . . . just in their own favor." The young man looked back to the mob and shook his head. "Because the Palestinians do not believe in the principles of Jewish return, they don't accept that God promised this land to us, as it is written in Genesis."

"This was never their land." Binny tried to test a theory he had heard his father say again and again. "They have been nomads, searching for their own Holy Land for . . . forever."

The young man smiled patiently and scratched his head. "Not quite," he said.

"It is true, though," Binny persisted. He had read this. The Palestinians had not really found a home in this state. So how could they really call it home? They were, to his way of thinking, lost souls. They should live in Jordan, Syria, and Lebanon.

"According to your teachings," the young man corrected. "But . . ." He paused and tried to think of a way to explain this. "If I'm playing a game with my set of rules, and you have the same game, only different rules, who's right?"

Binny blinked.

But their rage and violence was not something Binny could tolerate. He knew all too well the price the Israelis had paid for the Palestinians' anger.

"But I wouldn't come and destroy your home for having that game," Binny said, and the young man agreed.

"You are right. The way they are fighting us . . . this . . . is wrong. Still, for all the things they do to us, we can't keep running tanks into their homes." Again, he shook his head, and Binny asked how things might be done differently.

"Talking, man. Just talking. I fantasize that I might reach out to a group of Muslim kids and make them understand how poorly guided they have been all along. You know, just get people talking instead of blowing things up."

But it was no use. They would never listen. They actually believed in what they did as though it were the right thing to do. And when the Israeli athletes were killed for all the world to see at the Olympic Games, the Palestinians celebrated this horrible act.

The confusing part was the international reaction to that fateful day in Munich. While most of the world agreed that the Palestinians had acted horribly, some said that they had been driven to do this horrible deed. There were some who were sympathetic to the Arabs. Because Binny also understood English, he had read magazines that painted a sympathetic picture of what was happening to the Palestinians, and it was confusing to Binny how outsiders could not see things as they were.

"Couldn't we just have our leaders talk to their leaders and explain things?" Binny had asked his father years ago. "Maybe if we explained it to the Palestinians, they would understand this is our rightful home."

"My son." Raanan had put his hand gently on Binny's shoulder. He had shaken his head a little. "They will not understand. They see things only as they wish to see things. It is not right that so many souls should perish. I know it is hard to understand. I can't always understand it myself. It is wrong for so many to be lost in this way. But this is our land. This is a land promised to us, and it is to be ours at all costs. To steal or kill is wrong. You understand this, no? But this is different. The land was given to us in a sacred, most holy promise. It is ours to have and to hold. This is our belief. This is what I know to be true. At all costs." His father's view had never wavered.

Binny stood on the street, looking at a young man much different from his own father. This man still believed in his faith but hoped there could be talk between the two peoples. And for the briefest of moments, Binny believed the young man. He had hope. He opened his mouth to ask another question when a voice called out to the young man. His friends stood outside the café, waiting for his return. No doubt, they wanted to hear how his talks with the older men had gone. Binny watched after him for a moment then turned toward the bakery. He had almost forgotten his errands.

The streets were long and narrow, jam-packed with people, cars, buses, and carts. There it was again. That sense of urgency. It could almost be a smell. Somewhere, sometime, he had read that a person could smell snow—maybe from Robert Frost? He had read the poetic lines of winter coming and imagined what snow would feel like. Cold. Wet. But never had he imagined there might be a kind of smell of an event coming. Until this moment, he hadn't quite appreciated the idea. Binny looked around for a moment, trying to decide about the smell. It was something. It was a very faint, unidentifiable fragrant smell of something coming. But it was there and powerful enough to make him stop and look around.

The blast was so tremendous, it took several moments for Binny to fully understand what had happened. How long had he been there? He looked up at the ceiling and blinked. He was inside the bakery. He was on his back, on the floor of the bakery, still clutching his bread. He blinked. He had just walked into the bakery, picked up the bread, and walked out when the explosion came.

He heard screams from everywhere— horrible, high wailing. Slowly, he sat up and looked back out into the street of Kfar Darom. It was on fire. He was looking at smoke and people running in all directions. A car bomb! He jumped to his feet and quickly discovered he was barefoot. The blast had thrown him clear into the store and out of his shoes. For a moment, he squinted outside, looking on the sidewalk. His shoes lay undisturbed as though someone had neatly placed them there for safekeeping.

More screaming. Then sirens.

Binny moved forward. As he neared the doorway, someone ran by and kicked one of his shoes, spilling it onto the street. Binny darted out through four or five more people and grabbed his one remaining shoe. A darkness had settled over the street. Now he had his smell. It was distinct. Smoke. Gasoline. Burning rubber. Something acidic. There was also a different smell—pure fear.

People were yelling all around him. Some called for the police. Others for help, although he did not know if they were hurt or simply frightened. He could hear small children crying and the kind of wailing from an adult that could only mean a loved one had been killed. He didn't have to see anything. Just the sound alone told the whole terrible story. He felt sick. A horrible feeling began to grow in his stomach—death.

Had that been the smell coming?

He looked to his right. Not too far from where he stood, he could see a large group of people gathering. Their reactions were mixed, and Binny knew they were near the point of the explosion. He could see some adults holding their faces, partially covering their eyes but still looking upon the horror in front of them. It was too horrible to look at, too horrible to look away. Shock and disbelief froze many, while others went straight to work. The people of Israel had seen so much, they knew there was no time to waste. Binny could see men bent over, lifting objects, perhaps pieces of a car, off victims. He could see one man pointing, giving instructions to everyone about him until the police and medical units arrived. Another woman consoled a crying woman—maybe she was a victim.

To his left, he heard the sirens. A small police car screeched around the corner. He could see a man sitting in the back, holding a large medical bag. Binny stood back, watching the car fly by and wondering how one little bag would fix the disaster that lay before him.

Ashes began to fall like a light rain, creating a kind of fog. Binny looked up into the ashen sky and blinked against the falling debris. He felt a quiet numbness come over him. He couldn't believe this was happening. He couldn't believe he had been knocked completely out of his shoes by an explosion. And the sounds of crying children and screaming sirens reached only his subconscious. Instead, he focused on his hand. He had wiped it along his shirt, as he might had it been wet from rain. A long black soot stain smeared down his shirt, and he stared dumbly at it for a moment. He felt a quiet rage well up inside him, and he heard his father's voice as clearly as if Raanan had been standing right next to him.

"This is our land, and we will fight for it at all costs."

More than ever, talk seemed impossible. No one wanted to talk. Everyone wanted to fight.

3

Ahmy

STAKING CLAIM

THE sickness did come. Cholera took many people, including the ten-month-old daughter of a woman Hiba Aziz had spent time with. Maybe this was what made Abdel Aziz move his family again. Or perhaps it was the words of Mawlawi Azduk that night by the fire. Ahmy couldn't be sure. As soon as little Fatima was buried, the Aziz family was on the move. As always, they took almost nothing with them. The tents, blankets, and empty water can were left behind. Hiba Aziz smuggled a frying pan supplied from the U.N. beneath her clothing, and Abdel was allowed to take a day's supply of food in his pack. With that and the clothing on their backs, Ahmy and his family crossed the Jordan River again to get closer to their home and the enemy. Six other families traveled with them. Yet even though he was surrounded by people, Ahmy felt very alone. How long ago had he only thought of playing? How long ago had he wondered about his father's business? He, too, would have been a successful merchant in the marketplace. How long ago had he daydreamed of traveling to the ocean for vacation and wondered about sharks and whales and magnificent creatures he had only read about? How long ago had he read a book? Had it been so many years ago? Or just months?

He rubbed his face for a moment. He felt a little stubble and rubbed a finger over and over it. How old was he? Birthdays weren't something they celebrated. As they moved slowly along the hot and barren land, he thought of his age. What was it? Was he 13 going on 14? School helps a person keep track of such things. He felt older. He felt serious. The days of running and playing were so far behind him, it seemed a lifetime ago. Many times he lay awake to hear his mother's bitter complaints to Abdel that it was not right that her children could not be children, that her eldest lived in fear of losing another sibling. She could not allow him to run and play football with the others for fear that he might step on a land mine. For so long, she had denied him the right to go to school. She wondered at her own sense of responsibilities and motherhood. Ahmy himself thought it strange that not playing with others didn't seem unusual to him.

What would he play?

He ran his fingers over his face once more. How old would he live to be? Strangely, this was what he wondered about. Not how he would live his life, if he would journey to Mecca, or how his own family life might be as a grown man. He simply wondered how long he would live. So did his mother. As they journeyed across the Jordan River back to the Gaza Strip, his mother silently wept. She did not speak against her husband, but they all knew she did not like the idea of returning to such a violent hot spot. To her, it was no longer home. It was danger. She had not agreed with Mawlawi Azduk. Away from her husband, to other women and within earshot of her own children, she complained that they had already lost too many sons, too many husbands, fathers, and daughters. She could not agree with continuing the fight when they were outgunned at every turn.

"They pound on our doors and tell us to leave as though we mean nothing. If we stay, they kill us. When we go, they try to starve us. But at least we have a chance if we leave," she would say.

And when it was decided they would return to the Gaza Strip, she spoke against Mawlawi Azduk. But only so women and children would hear. "I notice that Mawlawi Azduk does not journey with us. He sends his foot soldiers but does not risk the certain danger himself."

As they walked along, Ahmy could feel a trickle of sweat streaming down the side of his face as the morning sun was in full bloom, still too young to hurt them but menacing enough to cause discomfort. Soon enough.

They headed for the refugee camp called Khan Yunis. Of late, it had been an Israeli target. There had been several uprisings by Palestinians lashing out against Jewish settlers. The response from the Israelis had been immediate. They had used helicopters to fly over housing complexes, firing down upon Palestinian residents as punishment. The Israelis claimed only to have targeted those they believed responsible for attacks, but it was all too common for innocent bystanders to be hit and killed by stray bullets.

It was true that Mawlawi Azduk did not travel with them. Ahmy wondered why. But his words had been powerful. Ahmy's mother was right, but so was Mawlawi Azduk. If they continued to let themselves be pushed off their land, the Israelis would never stop. The Jewish settlements would continue to grow, encroaching on Arab soil more and more until there would be nothing left.

Ahmy did have something to look forward to in the camp. There was the promise of school. An education! Khan Yunis had established several schools and marketplaces.

"It is a chance for the Aziz family to rebuild their lives," Ahmy's father promised his family. "Ahmy can go to school, learn, and teach us of the world today." His smile was wide and promised good things to come. "We will rebuild, reclaim what is ours, and prosper." He meant what he said.

Ahmy could not remember how long the trip took. In fact, there was not much about the long, hard trek he would remember. It was funny how the brain shut out certain information. His initial reaction to Khan Yunis was that it was a slum—narrow buildings stacked together with clotheslines hanging outside windows. Everything was a dull gray and brown in color. The streets, perhaps once paved, had been broken up by mortar shells and gunfire.

But children appeared to be everywhere playing football, or American soccer, in the streets. A ball, once fully inflated and leather covered, was flat and tattered. But it was a ball nonetheless. The children wore clothing worn thin from constant use. But they were playing nonetheless. So once again Ahmy saw his people living in slums. At least, temporarily. It wasn't a place of prosperity and hope but one of desolation and depression. There was a feeling of anger that hung in the air that Ahmy could almost smell. It was subtle but ever present. He would hear men laughing on the street corner, sharing some kind of joke, but no one was truly happy. In fact, the only thing that would bring Ahmy any sense of regularity or hope was his school. Daily, he would attend a school, and although the supplies were severely limited, he knew it was a place of hope.

◆　　◆　　◆　　◆

"Psst. Ahmet," a voice broke in, causing Ahmy to jump a little in his seat. He turned to find his friend Nasser Awad leaning forward in his seat and grinning.

Despite recent attacks on buildings, school continued, and Ahmy knew he was lucky to still have a desk to sit in. Nasser's little brother attended class where all the students sat on the floor and used half of a chalkboard. Chalk was considered a gift given to teachers from the United Nations and was received almost as warmly as food. His desk was a luxury. But as much as he wanted to learn, he was finding it difficult to study. The seasons had changed, and thankfully, the heat was lifting. The reprieve would be short, but it was a time Ahmy loved. He wanted to be outside, exploring all around Khan Yunis and beyond. He wanted to play football with his friends and—

"Abdul wants to go to the wall again," Nasser whispered.

While the instructor spoke of Arab relations between Jordan, Iran, Iraq, Syria, and Saudi Arabia, Nasser and Ahmy made their plans.

"Are you crazy?" Ahmy shot back, keeping low tones. "We are not to go there." But he knew he wanted to go.

"Are you afraid?" Nasser raised his eyebrows and grinned. Ahmy scowled at him and turned back to the instructor. He heard Nasser give a little laugh. Both boys knew Ahmy was in.

Nasser had been the first friend Ahmy made when his family came to Khan Yunis. He was the same size as Ahmy. Taller than most boys but very lean. Both kept their hair short against their scalp and had facial features so similar that many joked the two could be related. Abdul Hanoud was their opposite. Short and heavyset with a thick mop of black hair and glasses, he struggled to keep up with them in their adventures to the wall. But he was fun, smart, and always fighting against the Israelis. He had been in Khan Yunis since the beginning. He had buried a sister who was shot while standing in their own house. He had watched his father die trying to save another man—again, against the bullets of a Jewish solider. Abdul had more hatred toward the Israelis than both Nasser and Ahmy combined, and with a slingshot in his hands, he was a dangerous rebel. He couldn't run, but he could shoot.

"To see him?" Ahmy asked over his shoulder, careful to still appear focused on the lesson.

"Yes. The stupid little Jew," Nasser snorted. "You know he will be there again. He always is. He loves his little garden."

"I don't know. It's only a matter of time before we are caught," Ahmy said hesitantly. It was true. They had been lucky the crumbling section of the wall led to the garden. But the Israeli soldiers had been closing the circle around the Jewish settlement. Not just in Kfar Darom but all over. Since the most recent car bombing—one that Mawlawi Azduk had taken credit for—the Israeli military had become more brutal than ever. As much as Ahmy wanted to go, he needed to be careful.

"They are too busy going door-to-door," Nasser scoffed. "They don't care about us. They don't care about the garden."

Ahmy looked up to catch Abdul staring hopefully at him.

The Israelis usually attacked the refugee camps by air, firing upon "suspicious" people, but the most recent Palestinian retaliation had caused great anger in the Jewish settlements. Now Israeli soldiers began storming Palestinian homes, going door-to-door looking for bomb-making materials and guns. Although they didn't find much, they made claims of having great success—always trying to paint the picture that the Palestinians were terrorists.

Ahmy gave Abdul a slow nod. He would go back to the wall and see if that kid was there again. As much as he hated him, he was interested in him. Why, he couldn't say. While Palestinians were penned up in refugee camps in their own land and remained the overwhelming majority of the population, the Israelis walked around in more open, plush places. It was reason to hate a Jew. But the kid from the other side of the wall didn't seem to celebrate his stolen land like the others. He sat alone in the gardens, picking at the dirt, lost in his own thoughts. He was different.

When school was over, Nasser, Ahmy, and Abdul gathered their belongings and headed out into the street. A street once nearly vacant was suddenly filled with children of all ages running in different directions. But the trio of friends stood on the edge of the school steps, searching the crowd for Nasser's little brother.

"There!" Abdul pointed. In the middle of the street, walking side-by-side with friends of his own, was Mohammed. As soon as the younger brother saw Nasser, he sighed visibly. He knew the routine. Nasser, Abdul, and Ahmy would hand all of their books and papers to Mohammed with strict instructions that he carry them home for safekeeping. The boys would rather be caught by guards than risk losing a precious book.

"You go straight home, Mohammed," Nasser instructed. His little brother looked defeated.

"But—"

"You have our books. You go straight home. After that, I don't care what you do, but do not lose our books."

"Then can I go with you? To the wall?" he asked. Nasser whirled around. He was angry.

"Don't say that again. Don't talk about that, little brother! You don't know anything about that, right?"

There was a moment of silence, and Nasser pressed closer.

"Right?!"

"Right," Mohammed said dejectedly.

Mohammed nodded and turned toward home while Nasser, Abdul, and Ahmy headed to the edges of the Khan Yunis.

"Stupid kid," Nasser said under his breath, but he fooled no one. As much as Nasser loved the adventure, he knew it was a dangerous place to be and did not want his little brother near the wall. The wall was no place for a kid.

As much as the Israelis detested being so close to the refugee camp, they were just a stone's throw away. Literally. Of course, the irony of this was that this was the fault of the Israelis alone. The Jewish settlement Kfar Darom had already been settled as had Khan Yunis. A wide bridge was between the two peoples, but the Israelis pushed farther, always wanting to expand their territory. It was they who had pushed closer to the edges of Khan Yunis. It was they who had backed the territories together and, thus, made it so much easier for Ahmy and his friends to invade Kfar Darom.

Bricks poking out in various patterns of a partially collapsed building made a jagged spiral staircase for the boys to climb. Gunfire had eroded the building, making it uninhabitable and leaving gaping holes for the boys to slip through. It was its own fortress outside Khan Yunis.

As they reached the base of the abandoned building, they looked around once more for Israeli guards or snipers. As they left Khan Yunis, they had pretended to be playing a game of football, passing an old leather ball between them in case anyone watched. They would take turns running, turning, and waving their arms as though they were signaling for a pass. In truth, they took turns looking around, checking out any changes in the structure of the building, any shadows lurking about, any cars, soldiers, or guard posts. Always, they had to be careful. But everything looked as it always had. The back end of Kfar Darom was not something anyone worried about. It was the gardens for the Jewish settlement. The Palestinian militiamen were most interested in the marketplace or living quarters. If they struck, they wanted to make sure there was someone there to be hurt. Attacking the Israelis' food source had been tried and had failed many times over the last few decades. The Israelis received so much support from the outside world, they would never be without food. The only way to hurt the Israelis was to attack them directly. This left a wonderful opportunity for Nasser, Abdul, and Ahmy.

The Jewish boy did not disappoint. As soon as the friends reached the top of a crumbling section of wall and peered cautiously over, they saw him at his station. Always, he wore a small round cap angled to the back of his head and held a small shovel in his hand. Squatting down near his plants, he poked around at the ground, pruned leaves, and picked a few fruits. For a moment, Ahmy focused on the tomatoes. Full, red, ripened. Those should be his. He imagined how marvelous they tasted. His mother would douse thick tomato slices in vinegar when they could get some. Olive oil came easily from Mediterranean neighbors, but vinegar was more difficult to get. Tomatoes were never available. Those should be his. Those should be his mother's.

He had heard that in the United States, tomatoes grew as easily as leaves sprout from a tree and were tossed aside just as easily. Ahmy had heard that Americans threw perfectly good fruits in their trash as though they were nothing. Fruits of paradise discarded so easily. Ahmy stared down at the tomato garden. He wanted the fruit so desperately.

"Look at him," Abdul hissed.

Ahmy looked to the boy. Again, he seemed lost in thoughts, and briefly, Ahmy wondered about that. Not that he could ever imagine being an Israeli, but Ahmy wondered how he would behave if he were to live the life that these people did.

"What does he think about?" Nasser wondered quietly.

"He doesn't think of anything of importance. He is stupid. He just sits," Abdul said. Ahmy wasn't so sure. But it was hard to understand why he spent so much time in the garden. Alone in a garden, away from friends and family. Was it guilt that brought him to this peaceful garden? Ahmy's father had often said that being Muslim was not a state of one's being but a position in life. It was an honor to be so close to something so holy. This boy seemed so peaceful and thoughtful. It seemed to Ahmy that he acted more like a Muslim than a Jew.

He had heard it said that the Jews believed they were the chosen people and that this land was their chosen land. They really believed that. But this was the land of Muhammad. The Dome of the Rock was the center of the world, the center of all humanity, and the place where the prophet had ascended to paradise. It was funny that with all of their studies and praying, the Jews did not know this.

Out of the corner of his eye, Ahmy saw Abdul raise his arms. He saw the elbow go high, and Ahmy knew Abdul's aim would be precise. The rock nestled in the slingshot was large, jagged, and chosen specifically to hurt.

"Hit him," cheered Nasser in a whispered tone.

"No," Ahmy said without thinking. Before he could catch himself, he reached a hand out, grabbing Abdul's slingshot. Abdul's mouth fell open.

"What?"

"No?" Nasser echoed in disbelief.

"You afraid?" Abdul asked, his eyebrows raised. If anyone was to be afraid, it should be Abdul. While his aim was great, he was too slow for running. Ahmy's little sister Summi could probably beat Abdul in a footrace. But Abdul's hatred of the Israelis blinded him to this fact, and he was constantly pushing his chances of being caught.

"He's not afraid." Nasser shook his head, pushing Ahmy back. Nasser shot a look of irritation to his friend. To protect an Israeli was the lowest thing you could do. To be fearful of one was even worse. And suddenly, Ahmy could hear his father's voice again in his mind. "Fear nothing except losing ourselves to the Jews." This, as Mawlawi Azduk preached, was the only thing to fear here on Earth.

Ahmy winced.

"Not the tomatoes. Do not hurt the tomatoes. I'm going to get those when I can," he said, and Abdul broke into a wide grin.

Binny

STAKING CLAIM

BINNY had smoothed the fruit with his fingers, gingerly holding the tomato between his palm and thumb. It was full, heavy, and almost too ripe. With the slightest nudge of his thumb against the stem of the plant, the tomato easily fell free into his hand, and he examined it. This fruit, he decided, was much like him. Perhaps it was why he enjoyed this garden so much and made it his own to tend. For such a plant to exist in this harsh environment was nothing short of a miracle. The same could be said of his existence in such a hostile place. By all accounts, the tomato was not meant to live in the middle of the desert. This plant, brought about by his own hand, was asked to thrive and grow despite all the odds. Binny marveled at the tomato for a moment, thinking not of its sumptuous rewards but simply how it came to be in his hand.

So much like his ancestors. In the beginning it was God's command to the Jews that they be holy and separate themselves from those who conducted themselves otherwise. This meant, Binny had been taught, that they must turn to themselves and rely on themselves. He had read in the Torah that God gave the Israelis a narrow land of milk and honey distinct from the desert areas in the Middle East. For Binny and his father and his father's father, this translated into one thing: Kfar Darom was their land.

But why here? It was a question Binny had asked his father and swore to himself never to ask again. The answer came with great passion and far more detail into holy scriptures than Binny had wanted to hear. In the end, he still did not receive the answer he had been searching for. Why would God place his chosen people in such a place where simply living could be so difficult?

"Had God placed his people in a paradise, our faith might never have been tested," said his mother, Elizabet. She saw that Binny could not understand his father's answer and made it so much simpler. "By placing us here," she explained, "he was forcing his people to believe, exist, and thrive in the most difficult of circumstances. It is a testament to the

Israelites and our determination that we might persevere.

"Much like your garden," she had said. "Do you think if unattended, that your beautiful garden could live as it does?" She had winked at him when she saw his eyes light up with understanding. "You nurture, tend, and care for your garden. Look at your rewards. It lives because you believe and you feed it. Your faith is the same."

Sitting in the garden, he turned the tomato over in his hand. It was truly an amazing thing. Without him, it could not exist.

He sighed suddenly as his mind shifted back in time to the marketplace, to the explosion. Two had died. Palestinians had taken credit for it, proud of what they had accomplished. Two mothers, one a grandmother, dead. As if this were something to be proud of. Raising a tomato in the middle of the desert and presenting it at the dinner table was something to be proud of, he reasoned. This was his contribution to the world and his family. This was his reason for being here at Kfar Darom and on this holy land. It was his will and testament that brought new life.

He examined the tomato again.

For centuries his people had been persecuted, burned at the stake, hunted and killed like animals, rejected at every turn, lied about, and misunderstood. And he should feel badly that he was living in Kfar Darom? No one had ever been kind to the Jews.

But his was a quiet discontent. Much to the disappointment of his father, Binny was not an emotional young man. He was not given to bouts of anger and loud aggression over the war that raged between the Palestinians and Israelis. He saw no need. His father did enough ranting and raving for all the men in his family. In fact, there were times when Binny was confused about his own feelings. The men of Kfar Darom did as much yelling as the Palestinians did. The names were different, but the ideas were the same. It seemed to be an argument without end. Although, there had been times when there appeared to be hope.

"So what happened?" Binny had asked his mother that morning. He had captured her attention in the kitchen as she prepared breakfast.

"It is not so easy to answer," she had sighed. "In 1996, there had been talk of letting a Palestinian state rule itself in the Gaza Strip and West Bank."

"Really?" Binny raised his eyebrows in surprise. It was hard to imagine his father agreeing to something like that. "Did people like that idea?"

"Some yes," she shrugged. "Some no. The Prime Minister of Israel had convinced many that this was the way things should go. It was believed that the two states could coexist and rule themselves independently. But then, as you know, the prime minister was assassinated by a fellow Jew who preferred killing his own leader to making such an agreement with Palestine."

"I remember that from school. We have talked about it."

"Yes, it was . . . terrible. And for a while, Jewish settlers were fighting even among one another. It was crazy," she sighed.

Binny thought of the young man with the glasses in the marketplace. He told his mother about the meeting and the young man.

"Yes, there are still those who oppose this way of thinking, but it is more civil. We are talking, which is important."

"But what happened to the idea of two states?" Binny asked, not sure he remembered this from his studies.

"Too much fighting," she said flatly. "In the end, this would only lead to the hardening of positions on both sides. Some suspected the Palestinians were behind the assassination. Our new prime minister was selected, and the violence soared to new heights. The Palestinians hate our new prime minister because he is known to kill Palestinians any chance he gets."

"Is this true?" Binny asked, and his mother looked past the kitchen, as though she were looking to see where her husband was before she answered. But she evaded the question.

"The Arabs responded with more bombings, more shootings, more slingshots, and rock attacks on Jewish settlers. There seemed to be no peace."

What Binny did know was that the Palestinians had made new friends in other countries who supplied them with machine guns and AK-47s. The slingshot and rock assaults still continued from school-age boys, but the men were now supplied with artillery. Within days of getting a new prime minister, two off-duty Israeli soldiers were captured by Palestinian police and then beaten to death by an angry mob.

Just as the Arab world hated the Israelis' new leader, the Israelis believed that the Palestinian leader was a liar and worse, an animal. He tried to cause riots and bloody battles every chance he got, using lies to incite his citizens. The Palestinians charged that the Israelis were on *their* soil and that the Israelis had caused great bloodshed to the Palestinian people.

"Ah, but it is not so simple," explained his mother. She rolled her eyes at this. "Do you remember? We have just attended the funerals of two women. Both mothers. My friends." She was quiet for a moment, and Binny sat, listening to his mother chop vegetables she would put in their meal. She was striking the wooden block harder than she needed, and he knew her heart still ached.

"Even the very soil where you have tended these vegetables," she said, lifting her knife and poking at the cutting board, "is a centuries-old graveyard for the bodies of hundreds and perhaps thousands of slain Israelis. On that score, the Palestinians have nothing to talk about!" Her voice rose. Briefly, he saw her wipe the side of her face. A tear. He didn't know what to say.

How odd to talk about scores. Just like in sports, everyone was keeping score. During the first Intifada, over 1000 Palestinians and 100 Israelis were killed. But in the 23 months since the second Intifada, almost 1500 Palestinians were killed, and the Israeli death toll jumped to about 600. The big difference was the use of suicide bombers by the Palestinians. They were doing their very best to even the score. It had become a huge sporting event. They kill us, so we kill them. They bomb us, so we bomb them. No one knew who had started what. All Binny could be sure of was this was a holy land promised to his people by God and that the violence had to stop. It was all he knew. But how to make it stop or how to make the Palestinians understand this, he did not know.

Carefully, he placed the tomato in a small bag he had brought along. This would be a good day. Binny could easily see four or five very ripe tomatoes just waiting to be picked. But as he reached out for another tomato, he felt the tremendous blast. Not again! Instinctively, Binny pulled his hand back. Still in a crouching position, he waited quietly. This blast had sounded close, though it was not inside Kfar Darom. It was just outside.

He would quickly pick the rest of the tomatoes and be on his way. But as he reached for another fruit, he heard the thud behind him. Binny spun around to find a young Muslim behind him, lying on the floor of Kfar Darom's gardens. For a moment, both boys were perfectly still, staring at each other. Binny recognized him right away. It was one of the boys, one of the shadows he'd seen before. He had never actually seen the face of the boy who hid in the shadows, but Binny knew the shape of his body, his head, and the manner in which he held his head. The image of the Arab boys taunting him and flinging rocks at him was burned into his mind and disturbed his sleep. Now suddenly one of them was there, staring at Binny with huge eyes, and it was difficult to know if it was fear or rage Binny saw.

Slowly, Binny came to his feet, still clutching his tomato bag.

"Ahmy!" a voice from above called down to the Muslim boy. Binny looked up, but the other boy never took his eyes off Binny.

Above, Binny could see two other figures that had stepped out from the shadows. Vaguely, he remembered those bodies as well. One tall, like the boy on the grounds before him, another shorter and fuller.

"Ahmy!" the shorter one called again. Ahmy, as he was called, stood slowly, looking nervously about.

"Ahmy! We must get out of here. Are you okay? Are you okay?" his friends called to him. Ahmy nodded. He looked back at Binny. Neither moved. Binny could feel his pulse racing. Never had he been so close to a Muslim boy. Binny had never been allowed to journey far from the settlements and certainly never out of the sight of his father.

"You have to get out of there! They are coming! They are all coming!"

Binny could see that Ahmy was surveying the grounds, hoping to find a way out, but, as far as Binny knew, there was none. It had been Ahmy's poor luck that the force of the blast threw him over the wall into Kfar Darom.

The blast. From outside the walls, they could all hear sounds of panic, much like Binny had heard in the marketplace. There were sounds of people running and calling for help. Soon, Palestinian police would arrive. Whatever had happened was outside the walls of Kfar Darom, and for that, Binny was grateful. Let something happen to their side for a change.

Instead, he watched Ahmy with interest. Ever since he was a small child, he had heard stories of what Muslims would do if they had a chance with a small Jewish boy. He'd had more than his fair share of dreams—bad ones. But he was not afraid. This boy who stood before him, who had taunted him and thrown stones at him, was the one who was afraid. All Binny had to do was call out, and help would come to him. If found in the confines of Kfar Darom's garden, Ahmy could be treated as a terrorist. With just one word from Binny, this boy could be gunned down. Arrested at the very least. He would be charged as an adult and then killed. Ahmy knew this as well.

While Ahmy stared at Binny, his friends pleaded with him from above to find a way out. They dangled their arms over the side of the wall, trying to convince him to jump for a hand. They would pull him up.

A siren sounded outside, followed by more sounds of women crying. Shouts and more shouts could be heard. Some for help, some giving orders, and still others of accusation. Neither boy had to ask what was happening. They had both seen the results of this war too many times. Instead, Binny cleared his throat and spoke in almost perfect Arabic.

"You should not be here," he offered. His voice surprised even himself. He was calm, confident, and loud.

"I know," Ahmy said back, slightly surprised that the boy spoke his language.

It was strange. Binny could feel a ringing in his ears. Should he run at the boy, ready to fight him for the funerals he had just attended? While that kid probably had nothing to do with the bombs that went off in the market, he surely knew someone who did. What would Binny's father do?

"You will be killed," Binny said, not sure where all this was going. Madness was happening right outside the walls, but time stood still for the moment. Binny was looking Ahmy up and down, taking in how he stood, his dark hair, his clothes and worn sandals. He was poor. He had not had many good meals.

"Ahmy! Ahmy! What are you doing?!"

"I know," Ahmy said back. Like Binny, Ahmy was ignoring his friends. He was staring at Binny with great interest.

The sounds from outside were intensifying, and Ahmy's friends were near panic.

"Ahmy, we have to leave. We will be seen. We have to get out of here. What are you doing? Are you coming?" It was a final plea from his friends.

"You will be killed," Binny said, again disturbingly calm. Ahmy nodded again.

"Ahmy! Now!"

More shouts from outside sounded closer and closer.

Binny moved forward.

It felt as though he were floating. He couldn't really feel his feet touching the ground. He couldn't feel the end of his fingertips. A humming in his ears just took over his body. It was, as he had heard said before, some kind of unreal experience. He was doing something he couldn't quite believe or understand. But before he knew it, he was standing right in front of Ahmy. Inches from his face. The enemy! He was standing toe-to-toe with the very boy who would chant, "Death to the Jews." There he was. Ahmy didn't blink. He didn't flinch or move away.

Minutes or seconds or hours ticked off the clock. Binny didn't know which. And later when he would think of it again, it seemed more like a dream. While Ahmy's friends called desperately to him, Binny laced his fingers together and pushed a leg forward, bending at the knee. For a moment, Ahmy looked confused. He didn't understand. Binny repeated the only thing he seemed to be able to say to his sworn enemy.

"You will be killed."

Not another word was spoken between them. Instead, Ahmy gave the tiniest of nods, placing a sandaled foot in the hands of Binny. He started to ready himself to be hoisted but stopped. Ahmy looked back at Binny and let his eyes trail over to the bag that still dangled by the handle on his wrist.

More seconds ticked off the clock. Ahmy pushed his chin forward, toward the bag. Binny blinked. Ahmy wanted a tomato. A tomato! In the midst of everything that was going on around them—something horrific, he was sure—this thug wanted a tomato. But what was more amazing, what would cause Binny to lie awake that night and rethink the entire scenario, was that he gave it to him. He broke the lace of his fingers, reached into his bag, and handed the Muslim two.

At once, Ahmy plucked them from his hands. He placed one in a loose pocket in the front of his shirt and held the other in a hand. No thank-you. No smile of appreciation. He took the tomatoes and then waited for his time to be hoisted up to his friends, to safety. Binny obliged, and no sooner was Ahmy standing in his hands than his friends reached down, grabbed him from under his armpits, and struggled to pull him over the wall.

Binny stood staring up at the wall, waiting for Ahmy's head to appear, to shout down a thanks. He could not remember how long he stood there. Ahmy's face never appeared. Instead, he heard the quiet sounds of feet shuffling away. Soon even that was drowned out by the sounds of agony and anger on the other side.

Binny looked back to his bag. They would have just two tomatoes for dinner.

INTIFADA!

IT would be hours before Ahmy would return home. There had been a few minutes of pure panic as he and his friends had picked their way down from the wall and through the rubble, trying to blend in with the crowd already gathered in the narrow strip between Khan Yunis and Kfar Darom.

It was easy to slip away from the wall and go unnoticed as more residents came from Khan Yunis, howling for revenge. Someone had died. This Ahmy knew instantly. Nervously, he looked back toward the wall, wondering if any Israeli soldiers would appear looking for him. None did. And for a moment, Ahmy wondered about the boy he had seen. He wondered about the boy who could have caused him great harm but instead helped him. He shifted the tomatoes in his hands.

Abdul pressed them forward, wanting to get a closer look and find out who had been hurt or killed. But Ahmy held back. There was a certain kind of reserved or detached bond he

had with his neighbors from Khan Yunis.
Perhaps it was because of what he had seen
from his own little brother's funeral or the
many times over he had witnessed families
grieving over a lost relative. Whatever it was,
he wasn't sure he wanted to know who had
been hurt or killed. It might be someone he
knew, so he would rather not know anything.
He had his tomatoes. He wanted to go home.
He was, he knew, lucky to be out of Kfar
Darom and back on his own side.

But whatever illusions he had of simply
slipping away from the crowd were over when
he saw the women running. It was how it
always was. A body had been identified, and
quickly a young boy was dispatched to find the
mother of the victim. Then she, along with her
sisters and friends, would be led to where the
body lay.

Soon the mother's voice echoed off the
walls of Kfar Darom, bouncing along the strip
and tugging at everyone's hearts. The sound of
a grieving mother was by far the worst sound
any human could utter—or hear. Ahmy
winced, wanting to cover his ears, but he would
not out of respect. Her anguish must be heard
by all. He stood perfectly still and watched.

As she made her way through the crowd, it opened up like a giant curtain. There had been so much noise, so many yelling and chanting "Death to the Jews!" but quite suddenly it became deathly still. Not a sound—no wind, no sirens, no words, no cries—could be heard as the mother stopped before her fallen child. Dressed in her black, flowing cover, she stood over her little one's body. For a moment, she forgot herself and pushed back the cover from her head. She did not care. No one did. Modesty meant nothing now. So many had stepped back and bowed their heads in sight of this that she seemed more than ever to tower over everyone. It was then and only then that Ahmy truly recognized her.

She had opened her mouth to break the silence and to let out the wail of a grieving mother, but Ahmy heard only the voice of his friend. It was also just then that Nasser accepted what he saw before him. His own mother. It could only mean . . .

Ahmy turned slightly, watching Nasser for a moment, not really sure what to do or say. Nasser's mouth hung open.

"Noooooo!" he cried and lunged forward, causing many in the crowd to step back, look over their shoulder, and move away even farther for Nasser.

It was Mohammed. Again Ahmy winced, remembering the last words Nasser had said to his little brother. He had instructed Mohammed to take their books back to the house. "Do not go to the wall." But Mohammed had wanted to follow his big brother.

This would be something that would haunt Nasser for the rest of his life. Mohammed had just wanted to follow his big brother and his friends to see what they were up to. He knew Nasser, Abdul, and Ahmy often went to the walls of Kfar Darom.

Someone cradled Mohammed in his arms and carried him back to the refugee camp. Mourners followed behind, saying prayers for the Awad family. Others, like Ahmy and Abdul, remained behind. While Ahmy stayed quiet, Abdul and the others shouted violent chants toward the walls of Kfar Darom.

"Revenge is coming soon! Revenge is coming soon!"

Gunmen fired bursts into the air while others lobbed rocks over the walls until the Israeli soldiers made their appearance at last.

It was an ominous presence. Decked out in fatigues and bulletproof vests, helmets, and fully loaded weapons, they slowly began lining up, one by one, along the wall. Their guns were poised and aimed at Ahmy, Abdul, and every last man and boy standing. Many backed up. Everyone shut up. Still, no guns or rocks were abandoned. The Palestinians looked up at the soldiers, and the soldiers back to Ahmy's people.

The Israelis could say whatever they wanted about their right to this land, but there was one thing Ahmy knew. It was staring him in the face at that moment. Since 1947, the Palestinians had been slaughtered like animals. He had heard that in the last years, over 175 Israelis had been killed, but almost 1200 Palestinians had been killed. That was the first Intifada. As he looked up at the Israeli soldiers, he could imagine them opening fire down upon the crowd. His people had rocks in their hands, and Ahmy was holding two tomatoes. They could say whatever they wanted to say about the war, but Ahmy knew the truth. He rolled the tomatoes over in his hands, looking up at the soldiers. The Israelis were vicious killers who would not even hesitate to kill a little boy.

It was that particular thought that suddenly made Ahmy's stomach churn. Mohammed. He had seen him only an hour before. Now he was dead. He would never see his face again. Mohammed would never carry their books again for them. It wasn't that he cared about the books. It was seeing his face. He thought about the sound that Nasser—not his mother, but Nasser—had made when he realized it was his brother who lay dead. Ahmy could feel a rage welling up inside again. He thought about lobbing a tomato right in the face of a soldier. It would be beautiful. Red juice would splatter all over the soldier's face and clothing. It might get Ahmy killed, but it was an entertaining thought.

Suddenly, there was a rumbling from the crowd. A few more took steps backward. A large figure appeared from over the wall.

"Shlomo!" someone hissed.

Shlomo Yissin. He was the Commanding General of the Israeli Force. His was a name Ahmy had heard uttered over and over again at the dinner table and at the meetings the men would have about fighting the Israelis.

But the General raised his arms in a peaceful manner. He spoke carefully in Arabic.

"Please go home. Please return to your homes. We want no more bloodshed today. We want no more bloodshed here today."

Although he spoke with raised hands, presenting himself in a peaceful manner, Ahmy noticed that no Israeli guns were lowered. With the simple wave of Shlomo's hand, his soldiers could easily take out two or three dozen protestors. Outgunned and outmanned, the Palestinians began to fall away, heading back to Khan Yunis and the funeral preparations for young Mohammed Awad.

"You," the General barked down at Ahmy, causing him to jump a little. Then he realized he was the only person remaining at the strip of land before the Kfar Darom wall. Still standing with his tomatoes, still wondering about the boy behind the wall and the way Mohammed had died, he squinted up at the General. "Do you know what has happened here today?" The General seemed almost sorrowful. Ahmy nodded but did not answer.

"Please. We want no more. Please go home." Then the General turned and disappeared from sight. Ten or so soldiers also left, but the rest remained on their new perches, keeping a watchful eye. They had heard the chants of the refugees of Khan Yunis. "Revenge is coming! Revenge is coming!"

The boy from the garden had been afraid when Abdul, Nasser, and Ahmy shot rocks at him from the wall days before. First, he had tried to back away, not wanting to take his eyes from his assailants. Then, fearing for his life, he had turned and ran. Ahmy would not allow himself to do the same. Slowly, he turned his back to the soldiers perched so high on the wall. He knew their guns were still focused on him. Slowly and deliberately, he made himself walk back to Khan Yunis. It was hard not to shiver. It was a terrible feeling to have a gun leveled at his back, but he would not let himself run.

But there would be no relief once inside the walls of the refugee camp. Overwhelming grief and anger had taken the camp hostage. If people weren't crying, they were screaming and swearing vengeance of the worst kind. Mohammed was a good kid. Most people knew him. He was always about, talking to people and playing in the streets. He was, as Ahmy heard someone say, "an innocent." If the Israeli soldiers would kill him, they would kill anyone.

Ahmy made his way through the crowds and headed for home. His mother, he knew, would want to see him. Always, she worried that something might happen to him. As soon as he walked in the door, she searched his face for clues as to what had happened. She wanted to know everything at once. Where had he been? Who was it? She had heard it was the Awad boy but did not know for sure. And she had been fearful because she did not know which Awad boy it was. If it had been Nasser, she knew Ahmy would have been close by. Ahmy was careful not to give too much information. He would not want her to know he had been face-to-face with an Israeli, much less have his father know he had accepted help from one.

Suddenly, she stopped. She looked confused.

"What is that?" she asked, staring down at the tomatoes he still clutched in his hands. Ahmy looked down at the tomatoes as though it was the first time he had seen them himself. He shrugged.

"Tomatoes," he said flatly.

"But where did you get them?" she wanted to know.

"From a man," he hesitated. Too much had happened, and he felt overwhelmed. It was hard to think clearly, much less quickly.

"A man? What man?"

Ahmy's mind went blank for a moment. Where could the tomatoes have come from? He could not let his mother know that he had been so close to the blast that killed Mohammed. Moreover, he could never let her know that Mohammed might have died because he was following his big brother and Ahmy. In fact, Ahmy had prayed that Nasser was too upset or too angry to realize that himself. The guilt, he knew, could destroy Nasser. He had seen it happen with his own father.

When Ahmy's little brother died, Abdel Aziz blamed himself for having left their first home. He should have stayed and fought. Even when Ahmy's mother told him this was foolish, he had still claimed it might have kept their child alive rather than having him slip away to the sickness. But the only thing that could have been worse than letting his mother know how close he had been to the Israelis' bomb was to have his father know he had received the gift of tomatoes from a Jewish boy.

He shrugged his shoulders again, stalling for time. He tried to act as though it were nothing, but his mother would not let it pass.

"What man?" she needed to know.

"A man . . . a peddler . . . from . . . the West Bank."

"West Bank?" Hiba's eyebrows shot up. Momentarily, the tragic news of Mohammed was forgotten. News from the West Bank, any news, was a coveted thing. Any news via telecast was always suspect. The people thought the Israelis controlled the media and made up stories to come over the radio waves. The most reliable news always traveled by word of mouth, and peddlers made an excellent news source.

Briefly, Ahmy had been relieved. His mother cared nothing about how he had acquired the tomatoes but rather what the peddler had had to say. Before Ahmy could think of anything to say, Abdel Aziz exploded into the house. It was necessary for him to touch the heads of all of his children and see his wife. He had been working in the marketplace when he heard the explosion. News traveled quickly through the camp, and soon all the stores were closed down. There had been no time to tell her husband that Ahmy had spoken to a peddler from the West Bank. Instead of talk of tomatoes, there was talk of Intifada! Meaning "uprising" in Arabic, this word had many connotations. The word or the meaning had taken new life again in the late 1980s and early 1990s when a powerful uprising among the Muslim youth caused them to resist the Israeli dominance in the Gaza Strip and West Bank. It was said to be a movement that had started from the bottom up. The youth drove the resistance. Now many of those same young people were married and had children of their own.

"This was when Mawlawi Azduk came to power," Abdel explained to his family over dinner. He spoke quickly. His eyes seemed to dance with excitement, but Ahmy knew better. It was his way of dealing with the grief and anger he felt. "We were strong. The Israelis responded as they always do. Always more guns. They began to invade our homes and move us around, always moving us so we could not regroup. But we have Mawlawi Azduk back, and today on the streets there is talk of Intifada again. For Mohammed Awad. Praise God, he will not have died for nothing. He will lead us, give us strength, and show us the way!"

Only when he stopped speaking did Ahmy realize how long Abdel Aziz had been talking about Intifada, the Israelis, and Mawlawi Azduk. For a moment, there was an uncomfortable silence. Summi and Madi were too little to understand what was going on, so his father looked back and forth between Hiba and Ahmy, hoping one or the other would say something. Instead, Hiba pushed a plate forward toward her husband and tried a weak smile.

She had neatly sliced and decorated one of her favorite plates with bloodred tomatoes, soaked in vinegar and spices—just as Ahmy had fantasized. But instead of licking his lips, he felt himself jump. The tomatoes! He couldn't even appreciate the beauty of the fruit. Its flavor would melt all over his tongue and leave a taste in his mouth that would last for hours. It could be truly one of the best treats he'd had in ages. But instead of reaching for the fruit, Ahmy sat staring at it.

"What's this?" Abdel asked.

"At first, I was not going to use them," Hiba said, shaking her head. "I cannot stop thinking of the Awad boy. But perhaps this should be a time of thanks. We should thank God that our family is safe and pray that he brings young Mohammed home." She wrung her hands, looking down over the tomatoes.

"Where did these come from?" Abdel asked, looking to Ahmy for answers.

"Ahmy," Hiba answered. "He spoke with a peddler from the West Bank today." Then to Ahmy, she said, "Try it. I know you are upset about Mohammed, but you must eat. Tonight there is nothing we can do for his family. Tomorrow we will be there." She stopped, trying to find the right thing to say.

"A peddler?" Abdel asked.

"I thought I wanted it," Ahmy said to his mother. "But I don't. I don't know how I could eat this . . ." It was no good. How could he have brought food to the table that had come from the hand of their enemy? How would he tell his father where it had really come from? Abdel Aziz was no fool. He would know no such peddler existed. Ahmy opened his mouth, feeling tears form in his eyes. His head was pounding from everything that had happened.

"West Bank," Abdel nodded, speaking to himself more than his wife or son. "That is where it is to take place."

"What? What is to take place?" Hiba asked curiously.

"Have you not been listening? The Intifada. Revenge is coming soon." He leaned forward and made a stab at the tomato slices with his fork. "Mohammed will be liberated."

4

UPRISING!

"LIARS!"

"Murderers!" came shouts from outside Kfar Darom. The Palestinians were enraged and would not believe what the Israelis were saying.

The official explanation from the Israeli Army would not be enough for the grieving people of Khan Yunis. Even Binny knew that. While the Israeli army admitted that it had indeed planted explosives in a sandbag placed outside the walls of Kfar Darom as a protective measure, they also claimed that Mohammed must have been tampering with the sandbag. Binny could believe this. The Palestinian kids were always running around, getting into everything. Of course, the Palestinians denied this was possible. What did they know? A Palestinian boy had come into Kfar's garden and no one had even known about it. That little Palestinian boy, Mohammed, probably had been playing with the sandbag, curious about what was inside. Whether he had been or not, it was just another reason for the Palestinians to scream for revenge.

Confused, Binny went to find the young man with wire glasses and jeans. This was not something he could talk to his own father about, so he hoped to find the young man in the marketplace again. Not sure where else to go, Binny tried the café on the corner nearest the bakery. Sure enough, the young man was sitting at a small table, reading a paper and talking to friends.

No sooner did he enter the café than he could hear the topic of their conversation. It was what everyone was talking about. Was this Mohammed kid a victim or future terrorist?

"But they do not help themselves," said a smart-looking young woman. Like her friend, she wore wire-rimmed glasses and jeans. She also had a loose-fitting blouse and matching hair clips on either side of her head to keep her bangs away from her face. "They have an argument . . . but blowing up schoolchildren helps no one."

"But from their perspective," another argued, "this is just retaliation for the crimes against them."

The young woman laughed. "Are you saying then it is okay to throw bombs?"

"Not at all. I'm just saying, most Arab nations refuse to admit that the state of Israel is actually a state. To them, we are imposters or trespassers. So with every ounce of Palestinian blood spilled, like with this little boy yesterday, there will be swift and harsh revenge visited upon the Israeli people!"

"Never mind that the Palestinians started the whole thing," shot another voice. To this, the young man Binny came to see spoke up.

"They would not accept that. To their way of thinking, they were here first. We started it by coming in and taking over." A few heads nodded. "Does this make it okay to blow up buses and kill innocent people? Of course not. But to them, they would claim that they are the true victims."

"Shimon," said a friend. Binny took note of the young man's name, repeating it to himself. "I can't accept this. Whether you like something or not, agree with something or not, you can't condone suicide bombers. You just can't." The other man looked around to his group of friends, hoping for support. "We didn't just fall out of the sky here. Our people have fought hard for decades, against climate, world pressure, and suicide bombers. Are we supposed to bow our heads and leave?"

Quietly, Binny pulled out a chair from the nearest vacant table and sat down, never letting his eyes leave Shimon. He seemed to be the leader of this informal get-together. Maybe he would have answers for some of Binny's questions.

Binny decided to inch more closely and try to catch Shimon's attention, but before he could even move and before Shimon could respond to his friend, another young man burst into the café, holding a paper in his hand. Everyone within the café jumped. For anyone to enter a room in this way was cause for alarm. All eyes were upon him as he doubled over a little, trying to catch his breath.

"Today . . . this morning," he panted. "More . . . shootings." He shook his head helplessly and handed the paper to someone else. He was unable to speak. The young woman who first spoke to Shimon took the paper and read. Her voice was not particularly loud, but as she read, all other noise stopped. No one spoke, moved, or breathed.

"Revenge. The Palestinians, once again, have made good on their promise to avenge the young boy's death," she read. She sighed heavily and read on. "A lone Palestinian sniper armed with several guns opened fire on an

Israeli military checkpoint in the West Bank in the early hours, killing ten people. Seven were soldiers." She stopped for a moment and looked around. Binny did as well. People fell back against the chairs, lost in their own thoughts. On the very day that the Palestinians were to bury the young boy killed in Khan Yunis, the Israelis would now be preparing funerals of their own.

"In retaliation for the soldiers' deaths, Israeli Army Chief Shlomo Yissin promised for more pressure from Israel's army." Binny swallowed hard. He knew what this meant, and briefly he gave thanks that it had not happened in or near the Gaza Strip.

"The sniper had positioned himself on a ridge some 75 yards above the remote Israeli army checkpoint, next to an old British colonial police station in the Valley of the Thieves, north of the West Bank town of Ramallah and near the Jewish settlement of Ofra."

Binny was familiar with the settlement. Although he had never been there to see it himself, he had met two other boys from the settlement—two boys who had come to Kfar Darom for a celebration. He liked the boy his age very much and spent much of the evening talking to him. He had been critical of Kfar Darom for its rather flat, colorless environment. Ofra was located down in a valley, surrounded by terraced olive groves. Ofra was colorful and fruitful. Also, because it was in the valley, it was easy to attack.

The young woman read on.

"The gunman used a telescopic sight on a semiautomatic weapon that he used to fire upon the unsuspecting soldiers and civilians. In the early morning, as the soldiers were letting settlers past the checkpoint into Ofra, the gunman opened fire. One by one, he shot at his targets." Several sighs interrupted her reading, and for a moment, she stopped, letting everyone digest this awful news.

"As each solider fell, others would come out from behind blockades to pull their comrade to safety. The gunman simply waited to pick them off. The entire attack lasted almost half an hour before backup arrived and chased the terrorist away." She stopped. For a moment, everyone could only stare at her, waiting for her to read more, but there was nothing else.

Perhaps it was the fact that soldiers had been killed in this attack that made it so much more difficult to accept. The Israeli Force was known for its discipline and efficiency. It was said to be one of the most capable in the world. It was one reason in the midst of all the war and violence, surrounded by Arabs and Muslims, that the Israeli people were never *really* afraid. The Palestinians themselves recognized the power of the Israeli Army. Still, the Palestinians had promised more confrontation and more bloodshed.

"You were saying, Shimon," one of the men said toward Shimon. His voice dripped angry sarcasm. He turned toward the others. "You see, there is—"

The man who had run into the café finally stood. Having caught his breath, he waved to everyone to capture their attention.

"There is more. Soldiers have investigated where the shots came from. They are saying that all that was found from where the gunman lay were shell casings. Who he was or where he came from, the army could not be sure."

"But we all know . . . don't we?" the young woman forced a smile, and there was great muttering throughout the café. A terrible feeling grew inside Binny's stomach. While he hadn't been afraid of the Palestinian boy who came over the wall, he hadn't liked the idea that he got into Kfar Darom so easily. Binny was alarmed that his people made such easy targets. And it occurred to him that he should tell his father about the boy in the garden. He had thought about it many times. He had every reason to tell. The safety of his family, his neighbors, and the entire settlement might rest on knowing about the boy in the garden. Still, for some reason, he kept quiet.

For the next hour, Binny sat quietly at his small table, listening to the hot debates between Shimon and his friends. As the news spread throughout the settlement, more and more young people piled into the café.

Someone said that outside, across the strip between Kfar Darom and Khan Yunis, there was cheering. Celebration. Word had also reached the residents of Khan Yunis that one of their own had killed many Israeli soldiers— men who had families, perhaps small children of their own—and they cheered in celebration of the brutal deaths. Binny turned and looked out the window, but all he saw were the solemn faces of his own people. Still, he imagined what the celebration in Khan Yunis would look like. Somewhere in there, he imagined the boy from the garden. The very boy he had given a tomato to. Ahmy was his name. Binny squeezed his eyes shut for a moment, trying to get that picture out of his head. Little kids would be celebrating too.

The voice of the young woman caught Binny's attention.

"They don't know why they are singing and dancing. They just imitate the adults. In fact, we have to remember that this is how and why all of this is happening."

"Each father teaches each son that this is how things should be," Shimon cut in, and many people nodded. Still, others were not satisfied and shouted for threats and revenge. There was nothing left to hear. At least, nothing Binny wanted to hear, and he quietly retreated from the café and started home.

As he walked along the streets, he imagined how his father was taking this news. He was, Binny knew, furious. And, like some of the people in the café, he would be yelling about conquering and taking. Binny thought about his scriptures, about life and living. Neither could understand the other, so Binny always thought it best to stay out of his father's way. Rather than go home, he decided to go to the gardens.

There had been a growing sentiment among the youth in Israel that the Palestinians had been treated poorly. All Israelis had seen Palestinians routinely stopped by Israeli forces, having their bags and personal clothing checked for any kind of weapon. It was why Binny had hoped to talk to Shimon. He was sure Shimon would agree with him that this was unfair to most Palestinians. But the older generations, like Binny's father, would not concede any empathy toward the Palestinians. "They are barbaric," Raanan would say repeatedly, but Binny could see little difference between what the Israelis and Palestinians were doing to each other.

Binny could see clusters of people, all talking about the news. Tension was escalating. The world seemed as though it were turning upside down. It had gotten so that a person could not simply go to the market for flour without looking over his or her shoulder. A suspicious-looking person sitting alone on a bus or walking too quickly down the street made people stare and wonder. No one was above suspicion. In the past, Palestinians had used young boys to carry out suicide missions. Suddenly, even children could be menacing.

A man outside the bakery shook his fists and shouted to no one in particular. "It is a victory for the Israelis!" He held a small portable radio in his hands. "Shlomo Yissin has just ordered Israeli attack helicopters to fly over Palestinian refugee camps, firing off two missiles into *suspicious* quarters."

A few people gathered around him to listen, and Binny slowed his pace. "He has also ordered tanks to enter the refugee camps," the baker roared, and some whoops came from the growing crowd.

Binny had a clear picture in his mind. Women and children would be running from the monstrous vehicles while teenage boys and young men tried recklessly to stand their ground and lob rocks and bottles at them. More people stopped to hear the news. For his part, Binny had heard enough.

As he turned the corner from the market, it seemed suddenly deserted. With this new information, most people would go home and stay inside for the day. There was no telling what more was to come in retaliation for the missile attacks. It was easy enough for Binny to walk through the streets and turn behind a row of newly built apartments, taking a narrow passageway to the Kfar Darom gardens. He called it "the gardens" when, in fact, it was a large acreage parceled out to different families.

Each family was responsible for their own plots, but most communities agreed upon certain fruits or vegetables and shared. For reasons he couldn't quite explain, Binny had always loved the tomato. There was something so amazing about the fruit that he loved to tend. It was a healthful fruit, perhaps one the healthiest in all the gardens. But it was more than just nutrition that inspired Binny. The tomato was a noble plant, having been around for centuries, deeply rooted in religious history. Some had argued that the tomato was one of the first fruits to nourish human beings!

Binny walked into the garden, stopping at the entrance to look around. He scanned the tops of the wall and the surrounding areas to see if anyone—Israeli or Palestinian—was about. He saw no one. Already, the sun was beginning to warm the earth, and the plants were responding. Early blossoms were reaching up for their dose of sunrays, while the leaves rolled out as flatly as they could, absorbing the heat. Too bad they had no reasoning mechanisms. Soon enough, the plants would be wilting from the intensity of the sun, and Binny would be pulling shades over most of them. It was something he did not just for his garden plot, but for others as well.

Strangely, the shades had already been pulled, covering over half the garden. Binny felt a twinge of irritation. No one else seemed to care the way he did about the garden. Why would someone pull the shades, denying the plants the early sun?

He had become rather territorial over the garden and his plants. He tended to think of them all as his plants, and he did not like the idea of someone toying with the shades or garden.

When he was little, he would slide under the shading, lie on his stomach between the plants, and read to his heart's content. No one would ever know he was there. Not his father, not other gardeners who would periodically stop by and talk loudly about the day's events, never knowing he was listening to every word they said. He had heard a great deal of idle gossip—some of which he even passed along to his mother. And he could remember a time, not many years ago, when there had been another outbreak of violence much like what was happening on this day. Binny had slid under the tarp, lying beside the tomato plants, and listened to missiles rocketing through Khan Yunis. He could hear people yelling, crying, swearing, and threatening. But he had been safe in the gardens and stayed there until things quieted down.

Binny surveyed the area. To his right, nestled in the corner where two walls met, sat a large rain basin, a cistern. Tin funnels collected any moisture that might accumulate overnight and trickle down into the cistern. Very little water was collected this way, so several men would carry in water by hand from time to time to replenish the garden water supply. Binny set down his bag and grabbed a watering can. Before he would sit and read, he wanted to give his plants a little drink. Always, the aroma from the plants hit him as he watered them. The smell of a freshly watered tomato plant was powerful. To some, the aroma was too overwhelming. It was a mixture of tangy spice and rich soil.

It was a treat for Binny to lie on a small patch of grass. Grass did not grow naturally there, but Binny had gotten ahold of some seeds from a merchant and had created his own grassy space. It was another reason he was so particular about his garden. He had watered and tended his grass just as he had his garden. The soft, plush strip of grass was his own little piece of paradise.

As he started to move toward the tarp in his plot, he thought he saw a movement, but not so much a movement as a feeling. An overwhelming and sickening feeling that he was not alone. His heart sank. Someone else was in the garden. Slowly, he lowered the can to the ground and stared hard at the tarp. It had been pulled over the plants for a reason—someone had wanted cover.

Binny stood frozen for a moment, trying to decide how to move next. It occurred to him that he could simply turn and run back though the passageway to the main street of Kfar Darom. Instead, he moved closer to the tarp. In an almost robotic move, he began removing the sections of shade, rolling them back to their original positions alongside the walls. Only six sections had been spread, and as

Binny removed each one, he could feel the person moving back a little farther. It would be when he removed the last tarp that he would come face-to-face with this threat. But he didn't care. It was too much! He was tired of the bombings and threats and killings. Having someone in his garden, taking from him the one place he cared deeply about, made him angry. Suddenly, he could understand the feelings of the Palestinians when they stood up against a tank, throwing rocks at it. Their efforts were pointless, but it didn't matter. It was a way of speaking out, of resisting.

Binny's hand reached for the last shade, unfastening the small hook from a bent nail in the supporting stake. He turned slowly, ready to walk back with the material and expose the enemy who was surely ready to pounce himself. With the sun beating down on the thin shade, Binny could see the figure clearly now. One person. Not particularly big. Male. A teenager. Crouching down. Binny's heart skipped a beat, but he moved forward, acting as though he had no clue of the other's presence.

Was he supposed to just wait to be attacked?

This was the very thing Binny's father ranted about all the time. The Palestinians were cowards. They ambushed people. Like the sniper who had killed the soldiers at the checkpoint. They would lie in wait for hours just waiting to catch one lone Israeli. At any other time, it would have been a terrifying thought for Binny. But on this day, surrounded by violence and with an intruder in his garden—his sanctuary—he was angry. He had taken so much for so long.

He took another step forward. He was running out of time and silently berating himself for doing nothing to prepare. The attack was imminent. Another step. He was almost upon the figure. He had been most fearful of a gun, unsure of how he would fight against that. But it suddenly occurred to him that a gun was foolish. It would alert too many people in Kfar Darom. It would be very difficult for the intruder to climb out again. No, this assassin probably had a knife or something. It was a horrifying and encouraging thought all at once. Another step.

Binny knew he was running out of time and steps. Within four more steps, he would be upon his enemy. An enemy in his gardens.

An enemy so bold that he would dare to lie among the plants in the gardens that Binny loved. The intruder was doing the very thing Binny had done as a child, hiding from unsuspecting visitors.

Binny charged. Without any more thought, he took two running steps, lifted the shade high over his head, and let out a small cry. He saw no face, no gun, and no knife. Just a figure. He lunged forward blindly, ready to deliver a fierce kick to the crouching stranger.

There was no plan beyond that. He was only thinking of bringing the enemy and his weapon down. He was thinking about ramming a fist into someone's face or maybe shoving dirt into his mouth. He was thinking about getting the enemy before the enemy could get him. But as the tarp rose, so, too, did the stranger. Binny moved in quickly, still yelling, and the stranger stood, trying to dive out of the way. But Binny had been too fast. He slammed into the other body, hitting it with such force that both grunted and fell to the ground. They rolled over and over the plants, which further enraged Binny. It was strange that in the midst of trying to locate the enemy's weapon, he should think about damaging the plants. But there was no weapon! Binny saw that. Instead, it was boy against boy, wrestling to see who would win.

Around and around they rolled. Then Binny felt a sharp blow to the side of his face, and he lay still for a moment—stunned. He looked back at the face that now glowered at him and hissed, "You!"

A DAY IN THE LIFE

KHAN Yunis was a town virtually shut down by the funeral of Mohammed Awad. There were just as many residents of Khan Yunis who didn't know him as there were who did. It didn't matter. Everyone wanted to be present at the funeral. Everyone wanted to touch his coffin as it passed through the streets, grieve with the boy's mother, and shout out their dismay and anger. Ahmy had not seen Nasser since they escaped Kfar Darom. His had been the last hand Ahmy touched when Nasser helped him up over the wall and down the jagged bricks. From the moment they recognized Nasser's mother from the crowd, Nasser had been swept into the crowd of mourners. Ahmy had thought of going to Nasser's house to retrieve his books. He really didn't want the books. It was just an excuse to see how Nasser and his family were doing. But there had been a sea of people going in and out of their home, so Ahmy decided to stay away. For a little while.

In the early morning hours, he sat on the edge of his sleeping pallet and wondered what he should say to Nasser when he saw him. And he wondered if Abdul had been around. He couldn't exactly say he was surprised that another person had been killed. The violence and anger among his people had been growing. It wasn't enough that the Israelis took their land. Now they drove tanks through Palestinian homes and camps in the middle of the day, fearing nothing and threatening everything. But it had been a surprise to have someone he knew so well, someone he had just talked to, be killed. It was a surprise because they had just left the enemy's wall and felt good about it. Had they not heard the explosion, they would have been laughing about their little visit to Kfar Darom. But everything had changed in the blink of an eye. Adding to their agony was the indignity the Israelis tried to place upon Mohammed, implying that perhaps young Mohammed was killed because he had been doing something wrong. Anyone who knew him knew this simply was not so. He was a good kid, always minding his older brother and parents. He was good in school and loved to play football. All he had done was follow his brother. The Israelis tried to suggest otherwise, and this was an insult that the people of Khan Yunis could and would not endure!

All night, Ahmy had listened to the mourners crying for Mohammed's restful peace. And all night he had heard the men. As far as Ahmy was concerned, the plans promised to bring more pain and suffering for all sides. Soon after dawn, word came that there had been a Palestinian attack in the West Bank. Israeli soldiers were killed, and the people of Khan Yunis celebrated.

Death in this manner was never a good thing. It was not that the people celebrated the actual deaths of these soldiers. It was what the deaths represented. How many times were innocent Palestinians threatened, questioned, or killed at the hands of the Israeli Army? Too many times to count. So to hear news that these monsters were hurt or frightened was cause for celebration. Ahmy was sure the Israeli soldiers cared very little about the death of Mohammed. They didn't care that he was a good kid. In fact, they tried to make him out to be something else just to make themselves feel better.

Ahmy rubbed his eyes and wondered what the boy from the garden thought about all this. Was there celebration when a Palestinian boy was killed? Did the Israelis think it a good thing when there was one less Palestinian in the world? Ahmy couldn't be sure about the kid from the garden, but he was sure other Israelis were happy.

He knew what the Israelis thought of his people. He had heard stories of how the Israeli soldiers scrutinized and threatened women and children. They tried to scare them, make them afraid to move about on their own land. This was, Ahmy believed, because deep down the Israelis knew they should not be on Palestinian soil.

Ahmy didn't know a lot about the outside world, but he knew right from wrong. He knew that this had been the land of his people and that it had been taken away. Since that time, his people had been treated horribly. How could the Israelis always cry about what happened between the Nazis and the Jews when what the Israelis were doing to Ahmy's people was no different? And Ahmy was sure that if the roles were reversed, the Israelis would be crying foul all over again, and the world would sit up and take notice. So why did these rules of injustice not apply to his own people? Why did the world not sit up and take notice when a boy like Mohammed died? Not *died* . . . was killed.

Ahmy had so many questions, and no one seemed to be able to answer them. Not his father, not Mawlawi Azduk. They knew historical facts. They knew the number of people killed and where and when and how. But no one could answer the really big questions like why this was happening over and over again and why no one outside his world seemed to care. Why was it really bad when it happened to the Jews in Germany but not so bad when it happened here in his homeland? Why did a kid like Mohammed have to die?

He used to think about how long he would live. He had come to grips with that kind of thinking, but he was not prepared to wonder about a kid like Mohammed. It should have happened to him or Abdul or Nasser. They were the ones who had pushed things by climbing the wall and throwing stones at the kid in the garden. Not Mohammed.

Ahmy stepped into the hallway of his dimly lit apartment building and reveled in the momentary peace. Once outside the building, he knew, things would be terribly different. Ahmy stood alone in the empty hallway a moment longer, thinking about how Nasser might look, what Ahmy might say, and how much he wished he could turn the events of yesterday around.

They were two different worlds: the quiet hallway and the teeming streets outside. As soon as he pushed through the doors, he was instantly overwhelmed by what he saw. It seemed as though every person who lived in Khan Yunis was outside waiting for Mohammed Awad to pass by.

Ahmy drew a deep breath and fought his way into the crowd and down the street toward Nasser's apartment building. That was where the funeral procession would begin. As soon as he stepped into the street, he was hit fully with the powerful emotions of everyone. They enveloped him. It was difficult to fully understand. There was a heavy feeling of grief and overwhelming sadness, as well as confusion and anger. There was a sense of urgency that made him push even harder against people, fighting his way to get to Nasser. With every step he made toward his friend, he had the feeling that he needed to get there even faster. Before he knew it, Ahmy was throwing elbows, shoving his way through the hordes of people. So when he finally broke through the wall of people outside Nasser's apartment building, he almost jumped when he saw Nasser. Suddenly, there he was!

Nasser looked pale, his eyes downcast and hair neatly combed. Nasser's hair was never combed. It seemed unnatural. Ahmy swallowed hard, standing uncomfortably in front of his friend.

"Hi," Ahmy said, not knowing what else to say. He coughed a little, trying to get the lump out of his throat. Nasser looked up. His eyes were lost and confused.

"Hi." Nasser tried to smile. Realizing how awkward this was, he laughed a little. He sniffed, looked around at the gathering crowd, and looked down at the ground again.

"I . . ." Ahmy stammered. "I just wanted . . . I thought . . . I thought that maybe Moham . . . I was thinking I should tell you I'm sorry. I mean . . ." Ahmy found it difficult to find the right words. He had practiced how he would talk to his friend and convey his condolences to the Awad family, but seeing Nasser changed everything. It was all so real again. He couldn't believe that Mohammed was dead. Standing before Nasser's apartment building with all the grieving people and seeing the anguish in his friend's eyes made it official. Mohammed was dead.

"Thanks," Nasser said. His eyes were empty, and Ahmy wasn't entirely sure Nasser had even heard anything he'd said, which was a good thing. Ahmy silently berated himself for not having spoken better.

Seconds dragged by as the two friends stood face-to-face, not saying a word and not making much eye contact. All around them, they could hear people assuring themselves and others that Mohammed was in a better place and that he would have a better life. He would be avenged, as well.

"Thanks," Nasser finally said again. Ahmy nodded.

"Have you seen Abdul?" Ahmy asked, looking around and desperately hoping for help. Abdul would know what to say. Even if it was his typical anti-Jewish settlement talk, it was better than the awkward silence between Nasser and Ahmy. But Nasser only shrugged his shoulders.

"I don't know. He was here. He said he would be back. He said . . ." Nasser dropped his head again, suddenly overcome with grief. He shook his head. "He said he had to get something or take care of something. I can't remember. He was acting strange."

"I never thought—" Ahmy started but was interrupted.

"Nasser!" a voice rang out from the apartment building door, and about a dozen people instantly moved away from the door. Nasser looked back to Ahmy.

"I'll be around," Ahmy told his friend. Nasser nodded his head and turned on his heel and ran back into the building to his mother.

"We are to begin," a large man said from the doorjamb.

Ahmy began to look around for Abdul. It was odd that Abdul would suddenly leave Nasser. Maybe he thought of something to give the Awad family.

A deep, soulful howl swept over the entire building, startling many who stood outside the door. Nasser's mother cried as she followed her son outside. Wrapped in a linen cloth, Mohammed's body was laid in an open, handmade wooden box that acted as his coffin.

Because he was a martyr, because he was a fallen child of Khan Yunis, his coffin was passed through the hands of every man and teenage boy who was tall enough to touch it. Ahmy stiffened as he saw the coffin coming. It was all so much more real than he wanted it to be, than he could believe it was. Hands reached up to take, touch, and pass Mohammed along.

It had been so busy and loud before Mohammed's body was brought out, and it was almost eerie to Ahmy how suddenly everything became quiet. As it passed by, Ahmy reached a hand up and let his fingertips drag along the side of the box. He felt his eyes well up with tears. He wanted to cry out how sorry he was, but he didn't. Instead of walking with the crowd, he hugged the side of the building and watched as the crowd began to make its way down the street. Nasser and his mother, dressed in black, followed the cortege. Ahmy could not help but think too much tragedy had already happened to the Awad family. Two years ago, Mr. Awad and his brother, Nasser's uncle, had been killed by Israeli sniper fire. Now this. This was such a terrible day, and Ahmy wanted to hide from it.

Ahmy wondered again where Abdul was. He should have been around to see Mohammed go by. Then Ahmy's mind began to wander, to question what was so important that would make Abdul leave Nasser. How did Abdul feel about all of this? Knowing Abdul, he would go back to the wall at Kfar Darom and . . .

Ahmy got a bad feeling in the pit of his stomach.

"No," Ahmy said out loud.

It would be completely insane.

But that was Abdul. He was so angry. He blamed the Israelis for everything, even when it wasn't their fault. And this *was* their fault. This was the worst thing that had happened to any of them. It was hard to imagine what Abdul might do, but Ahmy knew he needed to get to the wall as soon as possible.

His mind was reeling. He began to run against the flow of the funeral procession, panicked by what he was thinking. He was sure that he must be wrong. Abdul would not do such a thing. But by the time he reached the outskirts of Khan Yunis, his heart was pounding. He was going at a full run, praying as he panted for breath that he was wrong. He cut between two buildings and skidded around the corner that led to the open strip of land between Khan Yunis and Kfar Darom. He kicked up a little dirt as he came to a halt and doubled over, trying to catch his breath. It was important not to bring attention to himself if there was anyone else around. But the terrain was vacant. To his right, he could see where the mine explosion had killed Mohammed. Black soot still remained along a wall, like some kind of disgusting remembrance stain. Beyond that, Ahmy didn't look. He didn't want to see anything else.

Not ten more yards from that stood several Israeli guards. Ahmy drew in his breath and stepped back against a building while he decided what to do. He squeezed his eyes shut and muttered to himself for a moment. *What was Abdul doing?*

He doubled back, moved down the street past another apartment building then headed once again toward the wall. This time, he had a straight shot to the wall. As he saw the broken-up building and the bricks by the wall in front of him, he put his hands on his hips trying to catch his breath. He had almost decided he had been wrong when he noticed some black cloth gathered up at the top of the wall. His mouth fell open.

Abdul had gone back to the garden inside Kfar Darom.

6

A DAY IN THE LIFE

IT was the shorter, thicker boy from the wall. Binny recognized him immediately, although he had no time except to simply react to his face. Binny pushed up from the ground then hit the boy full in the face. The two were soon wrestling on the ground again. Was it not enough that he had come with his other friends to heckle and terrorize Binny? Was it not enough that he had shot rocks at Binny and could have easily killed him? But now he would invade his garden like a common thief.

His garden.

Dozens of plants were being destroyed beneath their bodies.

"No!" he yelled at the other boy. "Get . . . off!" He began to grab at the thug, jerking him violently by his shirt collar. But the Palestinian swung back wildly. He cursed and swore at Binny in a manner Binny had never heard. Over the years, he had heard the Palestinians shout things, but nothing had ever been directed at him exclusively. He had never seen such rage and hatred up close. This boy wanted to kill him. For a moment, it took Binny aback. And it was that slight hesitation that allowed the other boy to get his bearings again and pounce. This time it was Binny who was on the ground, knocked backward, out of the garden area and close to the wall. He had landed hard, crashing the back of his head into the ground.

Venom spewed from the other boy's mouth, using Arabic words Binny did not know. But he could tell they were not good words. As he focused his eyes, he felt a sharp blow to his stomach and another to the side of his head. Things began to spin. He knew if he did not fight back, he would be killed right there at the place he sought peace. Binny renewed his struggle, kicking wildly and hoping to throw the other off balance. Another hard blow to the side of his face only made things dimmer. It was becoming more difficult to focus, to think and remain strong. He wanted to yell, but his voice was gone. He was gasping for every breath, and he could feel blood trickling into the corner of his mouth.

For a moment, the punching stopped. Binny was able to turn and face his assailant.

The boy looked crazed. His eyes had fire in them, and Binny knew at once that the boy was trying to decide what to do. His arms were above his head, holding a large rock. Too large for the slingshot but ideal for what he had in mind. Binny stared back at him. Time moved so slowly. Or quickly. Binny couldn't tell which.

Vaguely, he heard someone else, but he could only focus on the rock held between the hands of the Palestinian. Suddenly, the other boy looked to see who had called out. For a moment, he looked confused. Binny opened his mouth. To call out? Fight back? Pray for mercy? He would never have a chance to know. Something large flew above his head, hitting the Palestinian thug hard. Someone had side-tackled the Palestinian off Binny. There was another "oof" sound, and all suppressing weight on Binny's chest was gone. He could breathe again—a little. He rolled over to the side, coughed, and squinted to see better. Beyond his feet, another fight was on. The Palestinian and another person. Binny coughed again, struggling to get to his feet. He must help. He needed to get the rock out of the hands of . . .

"You!" he found himself saying again. Binny's mouth fell open.

The two fighters stopped. The one they had called *Ahmy* was sitting atop his friend, having wrestled the rock from his hands.

"What are you doing here?" Binny demanded. It was insanity. The Israelis and Palestinians were in the midst of one of the bloodiest battles in years, and these two chose *now* to leap over the wall of Kfar Darom and help themselves to the gardens? It was true then. Everything Binny had ever heard about the Palestinians was that they were quite mad as a people. Crazy. Binny stood fully, looking down over them.

"Are you crazy?" he asked finally in Arabic. Both Ahmy and his friend had been staring at Binny, a little uncertain about what to do next. But hearing this exclamation from Binny seemed once more to incite the friend, and he began wrestling with Ahmy all over again. Ahmy held fast.

"Are you crazy?" Ahmy repeated Binny's words to his friend. "What are you doing here, Abdul? What are you doing here?" As Ahmy asked this question over and over again, he shook his friend so that Abdul could scarcely answer.

Ahmy was not finished. "There is a funeral going on. Right now! And we have been looking for you. Nasser has been looking for you, wondering where you are, why you are not with him. Why are you here? Doing what?!"

"Look at him." Abdul turned his head toward Binny and spat.

"I could call for help right now," Binny shot back, growing more worried again. "And you and your friend would both be dead. You are fools."

"I don't care about him," Ahmy ignored Binny. "I still don't . . . What are you doing here? Why? Why?"

"Did you see how he gave you those tomatoes?" Abdul asked. "As though they were nothing to him. Nothing!" Abdul practically shouted, and Ahmy gave him another hard shake to quiet him down. Still sitting on top of Abdul, Ahmy had not released his hands from Abdul's shirt. He looked as though he wanted to strangle Abdul.

"What do I care about that?" Ahmy sounded horrified. "We are burying Mohammed!"

"I know that," Abdul snorted and finally seemed to realize he was on the ground with his friend sitting on top of him. He batted his hands at the side of Ahmy, shoving him off, and Ahmy let him, rolling over to one side. Abdul sat up and stared at Binny.

"Mohammed died because we came here. And so many of our fathers and grandfathers and uncles have died just so that we still might have a place to live. Then they," and he pointed a finger wildly in Binny's direction, "come along and take all the land—the good land—and grow beautiful gardens for themselves while we starve. They eat . . ." At a loss for words, he waved his hands at the garden. "We eat sand, and he tosses tomatoes aside to the enemy like they are nothing."

Binny shook his head. It was not why he had done it. He had not been tossing them aside. That stupid boy would never know how much he cherished and loved tomatoes and all of his garden produce. To give something that precious and rich to the likes of them was very generous, but they were too stupid and ignorant to understand it.

Ahmy sighed.

"Abdul, you should not care about such things. Not now. We could get killed just being here. I think we have had enough deaths right now." Ahmy stood up and dusted himself off. Then he stuck a hand out toward his friend to help him up.

"Do you think he mourns the death of our friend?" Abdul suddenly asked, pointing a finger at Binny. For a moment, Ahmy looked over his shoulder toward the Israeli boy. He had wondered that same thing. He watched Binny's face and considered it. It was hard to know what he was thinking.

"That is it." Binny took a tentative step forward, unsure of how much he should say or how close he should get. Abdul shot him a hateful look, and Binny retreated half a step.

"What?" Ahmy raised his eyebrows. He didn't look as though he hated Binny. He simply looked irritated.

"It is what you said. There have been too many killings. I do care about that boy . . ." Binny said tentatively.

"You care?" Abdul laughed. "Isn't that nice." He turned back to Ahmy. "He cares." Ahmy frowned.

"I mean, I didn't know him, of course. But, I care that someone . . . anyone died. There is too much killing. Too much. That," he said, shrugging his shoulders at Ahmy and Abdul. "That is why I gave you the tomatoes. We need to get along. That is why."

The three of them stood in silence for a moment. No one was quite sure what to say or do next. Noises from the other side of the wall, presumably the funeral procession, caused all three to look toward the wall. Binny saw then how Ahmy had gotten over the wall. Or perhaps it was the way Abdul had gotten over and Binny just had not seen it. He studied it carefully, sure he had not seen that before. A long black cloth, what looked to be of the same material as cloths that many of the Muslim women wore, hung from the top of the wall, tied off somewhere to be climbed as a rope.

"And your friend is right again," Binny finally spoke, this time directing himself to Abdul. "You will be killed if you stay here."

Abdul furrowed his brows, looking at Binny in a confused state. He opened his mouth as though he were about to say something but changed his mind. He scooped down to pick up a small duffel bag he carried and peeked inside, inspecting his goods. He dusted himself off and started to walk over toward the black rope.

"What are you doing here?" Ahmy asked again. His voice had quieted this time. He did not appear to be so angry as just very confused. He wanted answers.

"I came for this," Abdul said, tossing his bag to his friend. Ahmy peeked inside to see at least a dozen ripened tomatoes. Binny did not need to look to see what was in the bag. He knew. He clenched his jaw muscles and rocked back on his heels, quietly telling himself not to be angry. Ahmy shook his head and looked back at his friend.

"For this? You came in here for this?" He looked over at Binny for a moment, saying nothing to him. "Look, I would have given you what I had . . . I didn't know . . . but this is just stupid. I can't believe you did this . . . on this day of all days. Does Mohammed mean nothing to you? Nasser?"

"You don't understand." Abdul snapped his head up, looking between Binny and Ahmy. At once his face softened. "I . . . those were just one of the things I came here for."

"Then what else?" Ahmy sighed. He had been unbelievably irritated, but as soon as he saw the expression on Abdul's face, he was sorry he had asked.

"To kill him," Abdul said. His voice was low, flat, and menacing. Ahmy looked over his shoulder to see Binny swallow hard. For a moment, no one said a word.

"But you are right," Abdul said to the Israeli boy. "There has been too much killing, and you aren't worth it. The tomatoes are worth more to me than your life."

"Abdul," Ahmy said quietly. He stretched a hand out, placing it on his friend's shoulder. "It is not our fault."

"I know it's not our fault," his voice shot up, causing both Ahmy and Binny to jump back. "It is his fault." He pointed at Binny and hissed through clenched teeth. Then his voice was almost pleading, and for a moment Binny wondered if he might cry. "He shouldn't have died." Abdul shook his head, staring down at his feet. It was an awkward moment in which no one spoke. Then Abdul sniffed and jerked up his head. He looked at Binny again with the look Binny was more accustomed to. There was pure hatred in his eyes. "It is a symbolic gesture, Ahmy. If I can't kill him, and," he stopped for dramatic pause, "I could, then I want this." He held up the tomatoes in the bag. "It is the bounty of a Jewish boy," he hissed, "that should have been ours. This garden should have been Mohammed's here on Earth, but he cannot have it. Instead, we will enjoy it."

Ahmy had been staring into the bag as Abdul spoke. But when Abdul finished, Ahmy looked up. His expression was pained and sorrowful, and Binny understood at once that Ahmy could accept his friend's explanation. In fact, Binny could accept it. For the most part. Actually, this was his land promised to him by God, and the fruits were a result of the labor from his own back and hands. But in principle, he understood what the Abdul kid was saying. Ahmy looked over his shoulder toward Binny as though he were asking permission, so Binny took a respectful step backward. It was his way of saying he conceded. Under the horrific circumstances of Mohammed's death, Binny understood why it had been so important for Abdul to steal tomatoes. For a moment, for the briefest of moments, there was a deep understanding that Binny found most gratifying. Then . . .

"And what about you?" Abdul looked over at Binny, and again hatred filled his voice.

"What about me?" Binny asked, surprised.

"You are just going to stand there and watch us climb out of here?" He was almost laughing at Binny. Ahmy turned to watch Binny's expression, wondering the same thing. Although, his was not an expression of hatred like his friend's. Ahmy was worried.

"Yeah," Binny shrugged.

Ahmy opened his mouth to ask why. The Israelis had been awful to the Palestinians. Why was this kid being generous? But before he could speak, Abdul laughed at the Israeli.

"Because you care so much," his voice dripped with sarcasm. The boy seemed to ignore this comment.

"But if I catch you stealing my tomatoes again, I will call for help." Binny looked over his shoulder toward the entrance of the garden that led to the main streets of Kfar Darom. "And believe me, there would be a lot of armed men here in an instant."

Ahmy bent a leg, much as Binny had done for him the day he fell into the garden, and gave Abdul a boost. From there, Abdul straddled the cloth and climbed the homemade rope until he reached the top. For a moment, he struggled to get his leg over the side of the wall. The bag of tomatoes swung around on the back of Abdul's neck, causing him to fight for his balance. Both Ahmy and Binny stood back, watching to see if he could clear it. Abdul finally rolled over the top and landed on the platform on the other side with a dull thud. A second later, his head appeared, and he waved his friend on. The coast was clear.

Ahmy turned and looked at Binny, but not for help. He was curious.

"This is twice you have helped us. Why?" he needed to know.

"It is just as I said or as you said. There is too much killing. It is wrong. Perhaps we do not share all the same beliefs, but we know all the killing is wrong."

Ahmy nodded, turned, and grabbed ahold of the cloth. He hesitated again, almost laughing at himself. He looked embarrassed or confused, and Binny understood it. He was having the same feelings. He was supposed to hate this Ahmy kid. He was supposed to yell for help, have him captured so that he would be severely punished for even thinking about coming to Kfar Darom. He was a Muslim! Binny should have threatened to have him killed on that very spot. If Binny were true to his people, he would have sworn vengeance for every Israeli who had been killed at the hands of the Palestinian terrorists. He should have killed Ahmy and his stupid little friend with his bare hands.

Imagine if he went home and told his father he had caught two Muslims in the gardens and single-handedly taken them down! He would be a hero.

But he didn't feel that way. And he could tell that Ahmy didn't either. Perhaps his friend Abdul did. But not Ahmy.

"Come on!" Abdul called out in a whisper to hurry Ahmy on, and Binny jerked his head a little, snapping himself out of this fantasy. He almost laughed at himself. What was he thinking? That he and this Palestinian might be friends? It was an absurd thought. They would never understand each other and never agree on the other's lifestyle. They would never be allowed to be friends in public.

"Can't you stop it?" Ahmy asked, completely taking Binny by surprise. Binny had begun to step forward, ready to offer his leg for a boost one final time, when the question came. He raised his eyebrows.

"Stop what?"

"The killings?" Ahmy asked innocently, as though Binny could simply raise his hand and suggest that everyone stop killing one another. Binny laughed out loud.

"Oh, sure."

Silence.

"Of course! That was dumb," Ahmy mumbled.

"Come on, Ahmy! Let's go." Now it was Abdul's turn for common sense. Binny shot him a look of irritation, which Abdul skillfully ignored.

"You speak Arabic," Ahmy pointed out. It was simply an observation. Binny nodded.

"I like to read . . . and study."

"Me too. When I can. We don't have much for reading," Ahmy had begun, forgetting again whom he was talking to. He might have said more. He might have said he wanted to learn to speak Hebrew for all Binny knew, but Abdul put a stop to their talk.

"Ahmy!" Abdul hissed, looking from one boy to the other. His eyes said it all. He reminded Ahmy that he was talking to the enemy, and Ahmy snapped this mouth shut.

But Binny knew what Ahmy was thinking. Binny had felt a surge of excitement standing in person, face-to-face with the enemy, with someone from "the other side." Fate had been kind to them because both seemed to be of the same age and rationale. Both wanted to talk rather than fight. They both wanted to discuss and understand rather than shout and threaten. But it was an impossible scenario. At any moment, someone could walk into the garden and discover the boys. Abdul was perched at the top of the wall, demanding that his friend hurry up. It had seemed the perfect chance to meet a Palestinian, listen to his views, and share his own. But time would not allow that to happen.

"You don't know anything about my people," Ahmy said. His voice was not accusatory or angry. It was stated simply. Binny had to agree.

"Not much," he mused.

"How can you hate someone you don't know?" Ahmy argued. And again, it was not in a confrontational manner. It was something Ahmy had obviously thought about a lot, and Binny knew he had been right about this Palestinian boy. They were so much alike, he and Ahmy. Yet so different.

"I don't hate you," he said flatly.

Ahmy seemed to think about this for a moment.

"But your father does."

"As does yours," Binny said back. Ahmy smiled at this, and Binny felt a real twinge of regret. So much in common; so different.

They continued to stare at each other for a moment.

"Ugh!" came from above them, and Binny looked up to see Abdul draped over the wall, looking as though he were going to be sick. "I'm not going to miss Nasser and Mohammed," he called down.

Without another word, Ahmy took a hold of the rope and began to climb. He was far more athletic than Abdul, seeming to walk up the wall in three long strides. With a slight hesitation, he was up and over the wall. Binny found himself staring at the top of the wall, waiting to see Ahmy's head reappear, but it didn't. Binny was unsure of what he felt. Regret? How could he feel regret for not befriending the enemy?

He chastised himself for the things he was feeling. It was crazy. It was very likely that Ahmy's own relatives were responsible for some of the Israeli lives taken since Binny had come to Kfar Darom. Ahmy was the enemy. Ahmy was part of a people who killed his people in the most cowardly way by using suicide bombers, lobbing homemade bombs into public places like restaurants and buses. They killed little babies and pregnant women. They just didn't care. All Israelis, including Jews and Arabs with Israeli citizenship, had grown accustomed to living in fear and had learned to scrutinize every single person they saw as a possible terrorist. The Jews had come to Israel because it was a land promised to them. They should have been there living in peace, but instead, they were thrust into a horrific war. Ahmy was part of that, and Binny needed to remind himself of that quickly.

He went back to his garden, surveying the damage that had been done as he and Abdul had fought, and sighed heavily. Many of the plants were completely wiped out. Some could be salvaged. He began looking around for sticks to help prop up some of the more damaged plants in hopes of tying them off and letting them regain strength. Even more upsetting was the damage done to plots that did not belong to the Peres family. He wasn't sure how he was going to explain this.

Binny crouched down by a damaged tomato plant and began driving a stick into the ground next to it, talking all the while to the plant. He believed that somehow plants responded to human voice. So he mumbled to it about what had happened with Abdul.

"Hey!" Binny heard over his shoulder, making him jump. He turned to find Ahmy's head over the wall.

Binny turned on his heel, still crouched down, and looked at Ahmy in disbelief. The guy had a death wish. Ahmy suddenly looked a little uncertain, and he tried to laugh.

"You could always learn about us," he offered. "I mean, if you really care."

At first, Binny wasn't sure he understood. Binny and Ahmy just stared at each other for a few awkward seconds. Then Binny realized that Ahmy had thrust his hand over the wall. A gesture. His heart pounded. Briefly, it occurred to him that this could be a trap. It was entirely possible that the Palestinians had concocted some elaborate plan to lure Binny away from Kfar Darom and then hold him for ransom.

But why?

His was not a wealthy family. They had no heavy political ties with the Israeli government or military. There was nothing special or extraordinary about Binny. He was just Binny. But there was something unusual about Ahmy that Binny had sensed from the first day they met.

Ahmy was like Binny, just from the other side of the wall. And here was Ahmy offering him a chance to see the other side. Binny had never been to a Palestinian camp, much less anywhere else. He'd always had to wait for other kids to come to Kfar Darom. What little he knew about the other settlements and Arabs he learned from reading or news reports. He had never really been allowed to go anywhere alone because his mother worried about him so. He had often felt so isolated from the other side of his world. But it would be a crazy and very dangerous thing to go there! The Palestinians were a much more volatile and dangerous people than his own. He would be killed in a most horrible way if he was discovered to be Jewish. They would take no mercy on him.

He looked back at Ahmy.

Still, Ahmy had been over the wall twice now, and he didn't seem to be afraid. Ahmy had done it.

Binny felt himself stand. He could feel his heart pound in a way he had never felt before. It was so strong that he could actually feel his ribs moving. Binny had spent hours and hours reading about the Palestinian people and their traditions. He listened to teachers and his own father lecture, always a little dissatisfied with the information. Now he could find out for himself. Now he was going over the wall.

6

Ahmy

THE STRIP

AHMY had had this feeling he couldn't quite shake. Who was this kid? He didn't even know his name. All he really knew of him was that he was the enemy. But there was something about him that made Ahmy curious. Hopeful, even. As long as he could remember, Ahmy's father had told him that this would be a war without end until the very last Jewish settler left the Strip since there was no reasoning with the Israelis *"How do you reason with them when they believe everything here is theirs?"* his father would ask, arms waving in the air. What little Ahmy knew about the Israelis wasn't good. Their army was fierce and brutal. Reportedly, it was one of the most powerful in the world. Certainly, it seemed impossible to win against them. And because of the power they held, they were able to stop Palestinians at any time, question them, push them around, search their clothing, and rifle through their things. Most Palestinians were helpless against the

Israeli army. And the Jewish settlers were not much better. They, too, were well stocked with weapons. Most, Ahmy had heard, carried weapons and were almost as militant as the army. They believed down to the very core of their being that this land was theirs. Never mind that people had inhabited it centuries before them; never mind that they were coming in and ruining families, businesses, schools, and homes. Nothing mattered to them but what they wanted for themselves. They were to be feared and loathed.

Yet this one kid wasn't what Ahmy believed a Jewish teenager to be. He had imagined that even a young settler would be cocky, arrogant, and rude. This kid was none of those things. He seemed quiet, reserved, and respectful. He could have yelled for help when he saw Ahmy and his friends at the wall of the garden, yet he said nothing. He could have refused to help Ahmy back over the wall, but he helped instead. And when he saw that Ahmy had wanted tomatoes for his own family, the kid handed them over. Not like they were nothing, as Abdul had said, but as a kind gesture. It was like a peace offering and highly unexpected. Ahmy couldn't help but wonder if there were more who felt and thought like this one kid. Maybe his father had been wrong. Maybe there would be hope to one day find a resolution and stop the fighting and the killing.

There had been much talk of something called the Saudi Plan, an idea from a Saudi Arabian prince who was also sick and tired of the conflict. For most Muslims, Israel was not a state. Indeed, no self-respecting Muslim would ever acknowledge that Israel legally existed. Everyone knew that the Jews had come in and stolen their land. But in the Saudi Plan, the prince proposed that all the Arab nations would agree to declare that Israel was a real state that would be recognized. In exchange, the Israelis had to give back the land they took after the 1967 wars. If accepted, it sent a message that the Jews had to stop taking whatever land they chose. Supposedly, it was a plan that everyone could agree on. But the Jewish settlers would not agree. They didn't want to give up *any* land. Now they were singing the same songs the Arabs had been singing all along. The settlers said they would not give up homes and farms. Never mind it was on the same land and in the same homes where Muslims once lived. The settlers were adamant that they shouldn't have to give up anything. And the more the rest of the world called for the Saudi Plan or the Mitchel Plan, named for a former U.S. Senator who proposed it, or any other formula for peace, the more the two sides disagreed. The Israeli side denounced the idea of negotiating in the middle of war, and the Palestinians promised that the war would continue until the Israeli government agreed to negotiate.

It was all a crazy mess.

Ahmy's father and many other men sat up late at night talking about the Jews' "conspiracy" and how the Palestinians could fight against it. The conspiracy was, they said, that the Israeli government was making the Palestinians fight by refusing to negotiate land they knew the Palestinians would fight for. And as long as the Palestinians fought, the Israelis could claim they were the victims and wouldn't ever have to give back any of the land they had stolen! Ahmy could not help but wonder what the Israeli kid thought about it. Unlike his father and the other men who said that Israelis could not be reasoned with, Ahmy had a powerful feeling that this kid could.

No sooner did his feet hit the ground on the other side of the wall than he and Abdul started running. They wanted to get out of the barren strip between the two worlds of Israelis and Palestinians as quickly as possible and get to the funeral procession to support Nasser. Abdul had the tomatoes in his bag. In truth, Ahmy knew the tomatoes really wouldn't mean anything to Nasser. But to Abdul, the tomatoes were symbolic and, if nothing else, brought him some kind of peace. They had given Abdul something to think about besides Mohammed's death. They had allowed Abdul to think about and focus on something that would keep him distracted and would possibly put him in danger again. Abdul was that way. He was always on the edge, testing things around him. He never looked back to see if Ahmy was with him. Abdul was focused on seeing Mohammed and Nasser.

Ahmy had taken three or four steps when he suddenly stopped. He stood still for a moment, watching the figure of Abdul disappear between two buildings. A small cloud of dust still swirled in the air where Abdul had made tracks. Ahmy looked back over his shoulder at the wall.

What would a kid like this Jewish settler think of a Palestinian funeral of a little boy killed by the Israeli army? That single thought tumbled through his mind over and over. Ahmy knew what the Israelis said about his people. They called Palestinians animals and savages. The Israelis had better clothing, food, and living conditions, and they looked down their noses at Palestinians. It was as though they thought Ahmy's people were living this way out of choice.

Ahmy turned and headed back to the wall. This time, he didn't bother to look around to see if any Israeli soldiers were standing post or doing walk-bys. He didn't care. He scurried up the bricks, pulled himself to the top of the wall, and peeked over to see if the kid was still there. He was. Ahmy watched him for a moment. The kid was muttering to himself and driving a stick into the ground, trying to repair the damage done by Abdul.

"Hey!" he called out, startling the kid. Ahmy saw him jump a little. The kid looked up at him. For a moment, Ahmy couldn't believe what he was doing. It was very stupid and could get a lot of people hurt if it didn't work right. But just like with the idea of climbing the wall in the first place, his curiosity overtook his logic. He really wanted to know what this kid would think of the way he and his friends lived. Before he knew what he was doing, he had invited the kid over the wall.

The kid's mouth just fell open as though he couldn't believe anyone was that stupid. Ahmy shrank back a little. It was a very dumb idea. Ahmy started to wave his hand, telling the kid to forget it, when the kid stood.

Ahmy could remember seeing things he'd rather forget. He had seen his father bury his little brother. He had seen someone die in front of him by gunfire. He had seen a car explode, and though he never saw them, he knew people were inside. Yet, he couldn't believe what he was seeing now as he watched a Jewish kid crawl up a wall to go to a Palestinian funeral. It wasn't until he heard the kid say, "I need your hand," that Ahmy fully comprehended what was happening.

The two didn't speak until they were safely on the ground and had hurried out of the open strip area to hide between two buildings.

"I can't believe you came," said Ahmy. He was doubled over, hands on the front of his legs as he struggled to catch his breath. His heart pounded, but it was not from running. He had invited the kid over, but now what? If they were caught, he would be treated like a traitor by his own people.

"First," Ahmy said as he reached out toward the kid's head, going for his yarmulke. The kid pulled back instinctively, covering the top of his head with his hands to protect the small, circular hat that rested on the back of his head.

"It gives you away," Ahmy said patiently. Finally, the kid conceded, pulled the hat from his head, and tucked it into the back of his pants. Ahmy stepped back and inspected the Jew. That was another strange thing about all of this. Here they were, sworn enemies. Yet to anyone else, they could have easily been cousins. Certainly neighbors. Neighbors within the same community. Their dark skin, eyes, and hair were very similar. It was true that there were many Jewish settlers who were very fair in skin and hair color, but this kid looked like any number of Ahmy's friends. Ahmy shrugged.

"I don't know your name."

"I am called Binny. Binyamin Peres." He stuck out a hand for Ahmy to shake.

"I am—"

"Ahmy." Binny smiled. "For Ahmed?"

"Ahmet," Ahmy corrected, and the two had another moment of uncomfortable silence as they smiled at each other. Both were thinking, now what? Ahmy caught Binny sneaking a peek down the alley toward the main street.

"You ready?" he asked, talking to himself more than Binny. He could not know what would happen to Binny in his own home if he was caught with a Palestinian boy, but Ahmy knew what would happen if he was caught with a Jewish boy. It wouldn't be nice. Especially on this day. Not only the army but every Israeli was held responsible for the death of Mohammed Awad.

Binny nodded. He was ready.

"First," Ahmy said, bending down to scoop up a handful of dirt. He threw some of the dirt on Binny, who seemed sparkling clean. Ahmy had to wonder how often the kid bathed. Clean was good, but too clean was suspicious. The dirt assault made Binny stagger backward, inspect his shirt and frown. He opened his mouth to say something but then snapped it shut and nodded at Ahmy.

Without another word, Ahmy turned up the alley toward the street. Ahmy was glad Binny was behind him and couldn't see his face. He could feel the blood draining away, making him feel a little dizzy as they neared the open street. This had been all his idea. He couldn't blame this on anyone else, and now that he had Binny with him, the idea seemed more insane than ever.

Was it sacrilegious to have an Israeli attend Mohammed's funeral? he suddenly wondered. What would Nasser's mother say if she ever found out? Ahmy stopped, ready to call the whole thing off and send Binny back to safety, when Binny moved around him and stood at the mouth of the alleyway. Ahmy panicked. There was no turning back. Before Ahmy could stop him, Binny allowed himself to be sucked into the crowd, moving along with the funeral procession that included what seemed to be thousands of people.

"Wait!" Ahmy yelled out and ran into the street behind him. Had this kid no idea what he was getting into? He acted as though this were a parade or something. It took Ahmy only a few minutes to see the now slightly dirtied white shirt moving along with a Palestinian crowd.

Binny was taking in everything. Ahmy could see that Binny was looking at all the different people and, when he could, at the surrounding apartment buildings and stores. They marched for another ten minutes until they had reached the cemetery, and the crowd began to fan out a little more. Ahmy looked around anxiously, hoping he would not see anyone he knew. Most of his friends and family would be up near the front, nearest to Nasser's family. Nearby, a store that had stood many years before Ahmy was born had been hit by Israeli missiles and was now a large pile of rubble. Ahmy tugged at Binny's arm and pointed toward the pile. Soon, standing atop the pile of twisted metal and broken bricks, they could see everything perfectly. Binny was able to see Mohammed's small coffin and how it had been propped up before family and friends. Ahmy watched Binny for a moment. Binny squinted his eyes, trying to understand the speakers as they stood up and shouted to the crowd.

"They are talking about what a good boy Mohammed was," Ahmy tried to help. "He really was a good boy."

"Did you know him?" Binny asked Ahmy without looking away from the gravesite.

"You know when I fell in . . . your gardens?" Ahmy asked, and Binny nodded. "The other kid who was with me. Not Abdul but the other. His name is Nasser." Ahmy sighed as he heard himself speak the very painful words. "That is, or was, his little brother, Mohammed. We think he was following us to the wall when it happened."

Binny looked away from the funeral for the first time and stared at Ahmy.

"I am sorry," he said. And he was. Ahmy could tell from his expression.

Ahmy shrugged his shoulders and looked back to the crowd. There wasn't anything else to be said to that.

"Do not cry for this boy," a man stood up and shouted to the crowd of mourners. There were many hushes, and the world became eerily silent. "Do not cry for this boy, for he was indeed a good boy and will be welcomed into paradise with open arms. Be happy; do not cry. He died a martyr, a hero, and he will serve us well!"

A raucous cheer went up. Homemade flags waved in the crowd. Ahmy winced. It wasn't that he didn't agree with what had been said, but he knew the speaker, and he knew this speech was not over. It was far from over. He knew that there would be things said that Binny should not hear. Ahmy stood helplessly, trying to figure out a way to tell Binny they must go, just as the crowd quieted down again and the speaker continued.

"Mohammed Awad has been made a martyr not by his own actions, not by the hands of his own people, but by those of the bloodthirsty Jews! Mohammed was innocent, but he gives us courage and strength to draw upon!"

More cheers.

"We should go," Ahmy whispered to his companion. But Binny could not take his eyes off the speaker.

"I swear to you, and I swear to God, that they will pay a very heavy price for this crime. For that is what it is . . . a crime! Another murderous attack on our young. They prey on us like the devil! We will continue our resistance until the departure of the very last soldier on our land! In a body bag or on the run!!"

A huge roar erupted from the crowd, and Ahmy could see that Binny was nervous for the first time. This had become much more than a funeral. It was a rally to promote revenge.

"My God, it will never stop, will it?" Binny asked.

"I don't think so," Ahmy said, climbing down from the rubble. Binny followed.

"Who was that man?" Binny asked. "That man speaking? Is he one of your leaders? Who is he?"

"His name is Mawlawi Azduk. He is the head of . . ." Suddenly Ahmy stopped. He liked Binny very much. He had had a crazy idea that he could learn a lot from this Jewish settler and that maybe Binny could learn from him. He had thought that maybe theirs could be the beginning of a friendship that could help save people instead of killing them. But Binny was also a Jewish settler. He came from the people who hurt and killed so many of Ahmy's own people. Ahmy suddenly wondered just how much he really should tell Binny.

The truth was that Mawlawi Azduk had recently become the leader of a resistance group called Hamas, which was a Palestinian extremist militant group that opposed all peace talks with the Israelis. While Ahmy didn't agree with everything Mawlawi Azduk said, he understood Azduk's motives. Mawlawi Azduk's entire family had been killed in an

Israeli attack. With so many friends and family killed over the years and having been driven from his own home three times by the Israelis, Azduk was simply no longer able to talk about peace with the Jewish settlers. All he wanted was revenge. He wanted an eye for an eye. And as the violence grew in the West Bank and the Gaza Strip, more and more Palestinians were beginning to agree with Mawlawi Azduk.

Ahmy didn't like Mawlawi Azduk's militancy, and he didn't agree with him that the Saudi Plan was wrong because it would say that Israel was a real state. Still, he decided not to tell Binny just who Mawlawi Azduk was.

"He is a tribal leader," Ahmy said. "But I don't think he has much more power than that."

Binny made an "oh" motion with his mouth. The boys began to double back toward Ahmy's house. He had hoped to show Binny where he lived before taking him back to the wall, maybe even show him the last remaining slice of tomato so Binny would know how much the Aziz family had enjoyed the fruit. He wondered about what Binny had thought of Mawlawi Azduk's speech, but he wasn't sure how to ask such a thing. He hoped Binny might say something on his own. But Binny appeared to be too interested in looking around. He looked exactly like a kid who had never been outside his own garden before. Ahmy was glad that instead of being judgmental of Khan Yunis, Binny seemed to like what he saw. He didn't care about the dirt or debris from recent missile attacks. He didn't care about the tattered laundry that hung on ropes between apartment buildings.

They couldn't be gone too much longer, he knew, but he hoped to take Binny to his house and let him meet his mother. Hiba Aziz had not gone to the funeral. She had said she wanted to pray for Mohammed from home. Ahmy knew better. She didn't want to listen to Mawlawi Azduk. Like her son, she did not believe that more violence was going to help, but her husband disagreed. For a moment, Ahmy began to feel good about this idea. For the briefest of moments, Ahmy forgot that he was showing a settler around his home rather than just a new friend.

He shoved his hands into his pockets and opened his mouth to ask about school. He wondered what Binny's school was like, what they taught. It was nice to talk about something other than Mohammed Awad's death. Ahmy's guilt was almost overwhelming. Abdul had gone after tomatoes to take to Nasser's family to make himself feel better. Perhaps Binny did the same for Ahmy. Binny had been very sorry about Mohammed's death. Ahmy liked the idea that by learning more about Binny, he might help make things better. Maybe one day he would be able to share some things with his father about the Israelis that weren't all bad. It was a thought.

"You!" came a voice that startled both Binny and Ahmy. Both had been so lost in their own thoughts that they had not seen Abdul standing with two other boys. Ahmy felt his heart stop.

Before he could say anything, the two bigger boys had circled behind them and were pushing them forward, driving them between two buildings and away from the street. Ahmy recognized Abdul's older brother, Abassan. The other kid was Abassan's friend, and Ahmy knew they were both trouble. Abassan had been kicked out of school over a year ago for his outbursts in class. Ahmy looked from the older boys back to his friend Abdul. But there was no kindness in the eyes of Abdul. He was seething with rage, and Ahmy stood back against Binny. Binny was not going to make it out alive unless Ahmy put up the fight of his life.

Initially, he tried the impossible—to talk to Abdul. No surprise. Abdul wasn't listening.

"I can't believe you did this," he hissed at Ahmy. "I can't believe you brought *him* here. He is our enemy. Have you forgotten this? He killed Mohammed." Abdul's shoulders were rolled forward, and his chest was heaving. His fury was so great he looked as though he might either cry or have a heart attack.

"You are a pitiful traitor," Abassan's friend snarled from behind them. Ahmy could feel the older boys breathing down their backs. Binny had gone pale as he realized that they were going to beat him to death. His body would be hidden so that no one would ever know where he was. That same horrible thought flashed through Ahmy's mind too. *What had he been thinking?* These were not good times. Everyone was nearly hysterical with grief and anger. And a beaten, dying Jewish boy in the Muslim refugee camp would get no mercy.

"He could help," Ahmy said pathetically to Abdul. Abdul rolled his eyes and snorted. "Don't you see," Ahmy kept trying. "He can help us to know things and understand—"

Ahmy felt a hard shove in the small of his back that sent him flying to the ground. He landed hard and skidded in the dirt. Dust flew into his eyes, and he was momentarily blinded.

"I already understand," came the voice of Abdul's brother. Their voices were so similar. Ahmy could hear the same kind of venom in Abassan's voice as in Abdul's when the subject of Israel came up. "I understand that you are a coward, a traitor, and a no-good Jewish-loving infidel!"

Strength can come from the strangest places. All of his life, Ahmy had watched rage overtake and rule people, offering them a power that allowed them to do almost anything. But fear was a power of its own to be reckoned with.

Before he knew it, he was on his feet again. He came up swinging at Abassan first since he was the largest of the trio. Ahmy's fist sailed against the side of Abassan's face. Abassan dropped like a stone. Ahmy instantly felt a throbbing in his hand, but he didn't stop. He swung the other hand at the friend and missed. Or the other kid had stepped back. But Ahmy was wild. He swung again and again.

He heard Binny call out, but it was too late to react.

Abassan had gotten up and tackled Ahmy from behind. Ahmy came down hard, this time with Abassan on top. Dust and dirt flew everywhere, yet through it all, Ahmy could see Binny wrestling with Abdul again. When those two had fought before, Abdul had landed on top.

Ahmy fought harder, rocking his body from side to side until he managed to throw Abassan off. He rolled over onto his hands and knees and delivered a hard donkey kick to Abassan's friend, who dropped to the ground holding his groin. This was no time for civility. Ahmy tried the same thing with Abassan but missed. Abassan was back on top of him, pounding hard at his stomach and face, punching him in every way he could.

Ahmy covered his face for a moment, trying to block some of the punches, and then kicked wildly with his legs, trying to reach over to where Abdul was. He felt something hard against his foot and knew he had made contact with Abdul.

Never in his life did he think he would kick Abdul, but then, he never thought he would be fighting for his life against him either.

Ahmy heard Abdul make a noise as he fell off Binny, and he was dimly aware of Binny getting the upper hand. Binny was moving fast, rolling on top of Abdul. Abassan's friend saw that same thing, and he stood again. Binny never saw him coming. Ahmy wanted to yell out to warn Binny, but he had no wind. He was too busy letting Abassan slam his head into the ground. Abassan's friend was moving in, and Ahmy saw his hand rising in the air. He had something in it, and he was going to crash it down on the backside of Binny's skull!

"Abassan!" Everything stopped. Everyone froze. Ahmy looked back at Abassan with horror in his eyes. He knew that voice. So did Abassan, who instantly let go of Ahmy and turned around.

"Mr. Aziz," he said apologetically. Ahmy's father looked aghast.

"What is going on here? What are you doing? What are you doing to my son?" Abdel Aziz stepped forward. He was accompanied by several men, all of whom were returning from the funeral. They were all from the resistance group Hamas. Abassan stood, dusting himself off and trying to look innocent. Abdul was not so timid. Ahmy saw Abdul wrestle to get Binny off him and spring to his feet, pointing to Binny.

"It was him!" Abdul almost shouted.

"Abdul, no!" Ahmy shot back.

"I do not care what is going on. You should have more respect than this. Is this the way you honor your friend? Is this the way you honor Mohammed Awad and his family?"

The boys stood still for a moment, each casting glances to the other. But Ahmy never took his eyes off Abdul.

"But he—" Abdul pointed again to Binny. And Abdel Aziz's eyes shifted to the new boy.

"I don't think I know you," he said flatly, searching his own memory for where he might have seen Binny. Abdul snorted out loud.

"No, you wouldn't know him," Abdul practically laughed, though there was no humor in his voice.

"No? Then how does my son know you?" he asked, a little suspiciously.

"He is new here," Ahmy pushed forward, brushing Abassan to the side and facing Abdul. "He is new here and heard about Mohammed. He wanted to see the Awad family out of *respect*." He practically shouted the last word at Abdul. "He wanted to offer a gift to the family, and I thought he should. And you are right, Father. On this day, there should not be fighting. There should be a . . . a . . . brotherhood. This should be a time when we reach out." Ahmy knew he was babbling, but he had to find some word or phrase that would grab Abdul's attention. They had been friends for a long time, and Ahmy could only pray that Abdul would remember that.

Ahmy's father nodded his head slowly.

"That is right," Abdel Aziz said, looking sideways at his son. He knew something was going on but wasn't sure how much he should intervene. He looked back to Abdul. "You have a problem with this?"

Ahmy licked his lips. He stared hard at Abdul, boring holes into the side of his head, praying that he not say anything.

Abdul looked back at Ahmy.

"Nothing," he said finally. "I don't care anything about this guy."

There was a painfully long silence until Abdel Aziz spoke again. He eyed all the boys and said, "Well, then, please be a little more respectful."

When Ahmy's father and the other men stepped away again, Abdul shoved Binny hard against the wall. "And if I ever catch you here in *my* tomato garden," Abdul said, spreading his arms out, pretending that he had something so lavish as a garden of his own, "I will see that you are killed." He took another step toward Ahmy and stopped again. "You and I are no longer friends."

Binny

THE STRIP

HAD Binny Peres been asked what he expected at a Palestinian funeral for a small boy killed by Israeli arms, he would have been able to describe the events that he saw perfectly. He had heard and read enough to be able to see the funeral in his mind. Still, seeing it in person was an amazing experience. It was one thing to see pictures or form mental images. It was quite another to see all the anger and grief. It was still another to see political banners flying and the raised fists. Watching people reach out to touch the casket as it passed by and bid farewell to a little boy who had become part of history was electrifying. The sights and sounds blended together in an excited hum in the back of Binny's brain. In fact, the only thing that kept him from actually feeling happy was that this was a funeral. The sorrowful expressions of so many, including Ahmy, kept everything in perspective for Binny.

He had scarcely been outside the walls of Kfar Darom before, and he had no experience in an Arab town. He had been places when he was a small boy, but he had no real memories of the places or events. He knew only what his parents told him. Kfar Darom had been his prison. It was funny to Binny that so many of the Palestinians talked about the settlers as though they were able to roam vast amounts of land, free as birds. Nothing could be further from the truth. While Ahmy and Abdul and Nasser ran off to have adventures of their own, Binny remained secluded with his books and garden.

The activities of Khan Yunis were, simply put, amazing. Even the rundown buildings and streets had a story of their own to tell. As they walked away from the cemetery, Binny had a chance to look around the inner part of the refugee town. It was very similar to Kfar Darom—just different in the way things were kept. Binny could also see that war had taken its toll. Although he had not seen it, Ahmy had told Binny that much of their original school building had been blown up. Thereafter, schools were divided into sections, putting kids and teachers wherever room could be found in the small city. It was a different world. So close, yet so far away.

Binny had looked forward to meeting Ahmy's mother. There seemed to be a connection between Ahmy and himself. Ahmy told Binny that his mother's name was Hiba, the Muslim name for Elizabet, Binny's mother's name. Binny had been curious to see what she looked like and even more curious to see if she would be able to recognize him as an outsider. As dangerous as he knew it was to be on Palestinian territory, it almost seemed like a game. He felt safe with Ahmy because this was his territory. He would know who to talk to and who to stay away from. It just seemed as if they were playing a game.

Everything changed when they met Abdul in the street. Abdul was flanked by two other boys Binny had never seen before, and they were large. They were older teenagers who obviously had been told by Abdul that Binny was an Israeli. The hatred in their eyes was unmistakable. They looked as though they wanted to tear his head off. Binny saw that Ahmy sensed the danger. He stood close by Binny, trying to talk to Abdul. But Abdul wasn't listening. Before he knew it, Binny was in another fight with Abdul.

Just as it had happened in the garden, Abdul dove wildly at Binny, wrestling him to the ground. It wasn't that Abdul was stronger than Binny, just a more experienced fighter. Binny had never been in a fight before the one with Abdul. Behind him, he knew that Ahmy was getting beaten up by the two older boys, and there was nothing Binny could do to help. Clouds of dust made it difficult to see anything clearly. With Abdul on top of him, he didn't need to see anything anyway. As they struggled, Abdul said hateful things to Binny, things about his parents, his family, and his people. He wanted to say things back, but he didn't. He couldn't. Then Abdul seemed to fly forward, and Binny caught a glimpse of Ahmy's leg kicking out. Binny didn't hesitate but dove back on top of Abdul. It was Binny's turn this time to pin Abdul down, and he derived real satisfaction from the expression on Abdul's face. Abdul looked startled and horrified at the same time. Binny had him down. He could almost feel himself smiling, thinking of the things he wanted to say back, when another voice called out to the boys.

It would turn out to be the voice of Ahmy's father. At the edge of the street from where the boys were, Abdel Aziz and a few other men caught them fighting. They were going home after the funeral service. Binny could see the panic on Ahmy's face. He did not want his father to know that he was consorting with a boy like Binny. If ever Binny had fooled himself into thinking he could be friends with Ahmy, this was a great reminder. They could never be friends.

Ahmy had gone pale, waiting for Abdul to tell Mr. Aziz who Binny was. But he never did. Instead, Abdul played it off as though Binny were from another Palestinian camp, as though he had come with his family for the funeral. Nothing else. It appeared to be just another fight among teenage boys.

"Well, then," said Mr. Aziz, eyeing Binny once more, "please try to be a little more respectful." Then he walked away, turning his attention back to his own friends. All of the boys stood in silence watching the men leave. Then Abdul turned on Binny. Although he joked about gardening, Abdul's threat was very clear to Binny.

"And if I ever catch you here in my tomato garden, I will see that you are killed." The two older boys began to walk away, but before

Abdul left, he turned on his friend Ahmy. "You and I are no longer friends."

Abdul's voice sounded just as it had with Binny. Abdul hated Ahmy. To Abdul and his friends, Ahmy was now a traitor. Ahmy could only stare in shock as Abdul brushed past him and disappeared around the corner of the old building. For the longest time, Ahmy didn't move. He didn't speak. He just stood still, looking after his former friend. Binny could see that his shoulders sagged a bit. Ahmy did not know what to think or say.

"I'm sorry," Binny said finally, trying to bring Ahmy back to the present. "I have caused a lot of trouble for you."

"It was my idea." Ahmy shrugged his shoulders. Slowly, he turned to face Binny and managed a weak smile. "Well, I guess you should probably . . ."

"Yes, it is late. I should be getting back."

The two stood awkwardly for a few moments, not sure what to say next. Finally, Ahmy led the way back to the main street, through the next row of apartment houses, and into the back strip between their two worlds. Ahmy stopped at the edge of the alley and peered out into the strip. Nothing.

"It looks clear. No one is around." Ahmy jerked his chin over toward the wall and squinted at Binny. "Can you make it over okay?"

"Yeah, I think I can," Binny said evenly, trying not to let his surprise be obvious. *Was this it? Was it over just like that?* He looked at Ahmy's face and had his answer. Ahmy looked confused and hurt from Abdul's words. Still frightened from almost being caught by his father, Ahmy knew he and Binny could never be friends. The risk was too great.

"Well." Binny poked his head out into the strip, saw that it was vacant, and looked back to Ahmy. "Thanks."

"Yeah."

"I'm sorry about Mohammed, your friend." Binny wanted to say more. There were things he had read about, things he wanted Ahmy to know. They were alike, he and Ahmy.

"Yeah," Ahmy said, shoving his hands deep into his pockets. "Thanks."

"And Abdul . . ." Binny squinted at Ahmy, trying to read his face. "I never meant for you two to—" But Ahmy waved a hand.

"It will be okay. I am not worried." But he was.

Binny lingered a moment longer then moved back into the strip and ran toward the wall. There hadn't been anything else to say to the Palestinian boy. Once he got to the wall, he felt exposed. He could feel himself arching his back as though he thought someone was behind him about to strike. He was light on his feet, climbing the jagged bricks two and three at a time until he reached the top. He didn't even hesitate to check the other side of the wall. He just wanted to be back in his garden where he could feel safe again. With a big leap, he was over the wall, landing hard on the other side.

Suddenly, it was a different world. He sat on a small patch of grass and looked at his garden. It was a thing to be proud of. He scooted backward until his back was flat against the wall and tried to catch his breath. It was a very different world where he lived, and he was thankful for it. He reached up and smoothed the hair on his head. His mother would be angry when she saw him. He was dirty. As he wondered how long he had been gone, he leaned forward so that he could pull his skullcap from the back of his pants, but it was gone.

"Abdul," he muttered to himself. He must have lost it in the alley when he was fighting with Abdul. It was lucky that Ahmy's father had not seen it. Binny rubbed his eyes, trying to squeeze out the image of Ahmy's father seeing the yarmulke and discovering there was an Israeli boy attending their funeral service.

"How stupid I am," Binny chastised himself. It was a stupid thing to go to Khan Yunis. He had been very foolish.

"How's that?" came a voice very near Binny, and Binny almost jumped to his feet. The voice laughed. "Oh, I am sorry. I see that you were alone with your thoughts. I thought you were speaking to me." Binny looked up to find an Israeli soldier, fully armed, looking down at him.

"Oh, no, I was just talking to myself." He squinted up at the soldier. "How long have you been here?" He was young. Maybe 20 years old. Binny could see that the young soldier had some pimples around his nose and chin and wondered if they bothered the young man.

"Just came in. New rounds. We are adding the garden. Extra security." He shrugged his shoulders at the boy. If he only knew, Binny thought. "This yours?" He motioned to the garden with his gun as though it were just part of his hands. Binny nodded. "Looks good."

All Binny could do was nod. It was only luck that Mr. Aziz hadn't seen the yarmulke. It was more luck that this soldier had not begun his new rounds in the garden just as Binny flung himself over the wall. He could have been shot. Worse, Ahmy could have been shot had the soldier been to the garden even earlier.

"Well," the soldier said, "be careful. We are on high alert."

Binny nodded his head.

In the days that followed, Binny realized just how dangerous it had been for him to attend the funeral with Ahmy. A 17-year-old Palestinian boy, probably not much older than the boys who had fought with Ahmy, managed to enter a Tel Aviv restaurant with a bomb smuggled in his backpack and blow up most of the café, killing several people and himself. Israeli missiles were fired into the West Bank city of Ramallah to punish its residents, killing two Palestinians. This morning a Jewish settler was shot dead in her car.

Because of the intensifying conflict, more groups were stepping forward to call for peace. But other groups became even more determined not to give in to the other side. Extremists were not just a Palestinian problem but an Israeli one as well.

Binny sat at the kitchen table and quietly read the newspaper. More violence. More killings. He read about a recent atrocity in which an extremist Israeli group claimed responsibility for blowing up an Arab school, killing several children. The Palestinians quickly fired back, successfully launching their homemade "Qassam" missiles from the Gaza Strip into a residential area of Israel, wounding three civilians in the town of Sderot.

The Israeli government imposed more roadblocks and more searches through bags and vehicles of Palestinian travelers throughout the country and the occupied territories. General Shlomo Yissin said they would continue hounding the Palestinians until they realized they had been defeated. But the Palestinian leader Mawlawi Azduk ordered his people to attack Israeli checkpoints and soldiers as a way to reject the government's acts of hatred against Palestinians.

Binny stopped and reread the last sentence of the newspaper.

Mawlawi Azduk.

He was sure he had heard that name before.

Binny could hear his mother and father talking quietly in the other room. Lately, their tone had been hushed, and Binny knew something was going on. Not just in his own home but everywhere. He could feel it in the streets, at school, and all around him. Tension in the Middle East was building rapidly. Countries from around the world, particularly the West, were beginning to step in. Most were urging the Israeli Prime Minister to back off the offensive, not be so aggressive with the Palestinians. And for a time, Binny had been inclined to agree. Something would have to give. They were all killing one another. It had gotten so that Binny was barely going to his garden. Bombs, guns, pain, and suffering. This wasn't a movie. It had become a living nightmare. People were getting killed because they wanted to go to a restaurant to eat or take a bus. People were living in terror of when the next strike might be. Where? When? How? Most of all—why?

He listened to his father's tone for a moment. Although he could not hear the words, he knew the talk was something to do with what was going on in the Middle East. His father was quite militant about the Palestinians, and Binny wondered if his father was part of the increasingly violent anti-Palestinian movement.

Binny sighed and looked back at the paper. It was just like a tennis match. Israelis had cheered when the army launched more missiles into the Palestinian leader's compound, collapsing walls and wounding many. But they would not celebrate for long. The lone Palestinian suicide bomber was able to walk into an all-night café in Kfar Darom where 20-year-olds hung out. A security guard was quoted as saying that he didn't think anything of the bomber when he first walked in. He had dressed in a way that made him look like an Israeli. But once the boy had taken one step into the café, he simply blew up himself and everyone else around him. It was amazing to Binny that this boy, whoever he was, actually thought he would be going to paradise because he killed and injured a café full of young, innocent people. Binny shook his head and put down the paper. He felt sick. It was hard to imagine that Ahmy could be part of that kind of thinking.

As much as Binny didn't want to read the news, he couldn't seem to stay away from it. He picked up the paper again and continued reading. All of Kfar Darom was in mourning. Yesterday's attack—the café bombing—was a horrible shock to everyone, but there was one young man in the café who was especially important to the Kfar Darom settlement. It had been his home, it was where his family was from. He had just been accepted to medical school in the United States, and he had sworn to return to be a doctor in the community. He was handsome, funny, smart, and well liked. He had been like a son to the whole Kfar Darom settlement. He was a spokesman for peace and education, hope, and prosperity. His name was . . .

"No!" Binny said out loud when he read the name. "Shimon . . ." He never caught the last name. He knew who it was. It was the young man from the café. Shimon was the young man Binny had believed might have the answers to the many questions he had. Now he was dead. Killed by Ahmy's people. There was a bitter irony that Shimon had stood up against his own people and spoke in defense of the Palestinians—the very people who would later kill him.

Briefly, Binny felt rage even against Ahmy. He had to remind himself that Ahmy had had nothing to do with it. But his father had. This, Binny was sure of. Ahmy's father and his friends were most likely connected to Shimon's death.

Ahmy wasn't like that, Binny told himself. Ahmy was different, which was why Binny had liked him. It was why—suddenly, he stopped. Thinking of Ahmy had brought him back to the day of the Palestinian boy, Mohammed's, funeral. Binny could see himself there again, asking about what was going on and who certain people were. And he had heard one man talk. He was a very passionate man, swearing vengeance against the Israelis. Binny had asked if he was a leader, but Ahmy had said no. Binny rubbed his temples.

Mawlawi Azduk.

That was the name!

Not knowing what else to do, Binny went to the café where he had last seen Shimon. The café was in shambles, very similar to the pile of rubble he and Ahmy had stood upon at the Palestinian boy's funeral. Binny searched the crowd of mourners for faces he might recognize. At first, he saw no one he knew.

Then, just as he was about to leave, he saw the young woman with the wire-rimmed glasses. She had been a friend who had spoken with Shimon when Binny had gone to the café in search of answers. For a moment, he thought about going to her, but what would he say? Her eyes were swollen from crying. Instead, Binny turned and headed home with one name pounding through his brain.

Mawlawi Azduk.

When he got home, Binny grabbed the newspaper again. He looked at the small picture that depicted Mawlawi Azduk shouting, his fist in the air. Behind him were a row of men. Binny squinted, leaning forward under the kitchen light for a better look.

"Abdel Aziz," Binny said breathlessly. Then, "Father!" Binny leaped up from his seat and hurried out toward his father. He waved the newspaper at him.

"This man," Binny blurted out. "This man, Mawlawi Azduk. Who is he?"

Raanan Peres' eyebrows shot up. He was intrigued with his son's interest in the current crisis, and there was no missing the anger in Binny's eyes. He glanced sideways at his wife before taking the paper from his son. He studied the article and its picture.

"He is one of the leaders of an extremist group that would have all of us killed if he had his way," Raanan said flatly. Binny already knew that. He leaned forward. "But does everyone know this? I mean, is it common knowledge who this man is?"

"Yes," his father started slowly, "to anyone who reads the papers or listens—"

"But what about to his own people. To the Palestinians? Is he . . . respected?"

"Yes," Raanan said, looking hard at his son. "He stands as a symbol to the people. He— why do you ask?"

Binny ignored the question, taking the paper back from his father.

"And what about this man?" Binny jabbed a finger at Abdel Aziz. Raanan Peres stepped close to his son, squinting at the picture. "Do you know who this man is?"

Raanan Peres shook his head slowly then looked back at his son.

"Do you?"

"No, but I have seen him before. I wonder if he is some kind of leader as well." Binny's mind was reeling. Was Ahmy's father part of the extremist group responsible for blowing up Shimon, the café, and the residents of Kfar

Darom? He had been musing over the idea
that Ahmy's father was involved, but he hadn't
really believed his father was a leader, that he
might be directly responsible for Shimon's
death! Binny could almost laugh out loud.
Here Ahmy was trying to show Binny a funeral
of a boy from his own people when Ahmy's
father was one of the biggest murderers ever.

Raanan Peres studied the picture again.

"Where?"

"What?" Binny gulped.

"Where have you seen him before? Here?
In Kfar Darom?"

Immediately, Binny realized he had made
a big mistake. But he also needed to know the
truth about Ahmy's father. Suddenly, it
became very important to Binny. *Had he been
a fool? Had Ahmy been lying to him?* He
thought about that for a moment. Ahmy had
lied. Ahmy had told him that Mawlawi Azduk
was no one.

"No. I mean, I don't know. I have seen
him, I know. I just don't know where." Binny
winced. "The paper, I think." He tried to back
up. But Raanan Peres' temper was rising fast.
Before Binny knew it, his father was dragging
him out of the apartment and across the hall to

the home of Ian Khatib. Mr. Khatib had been a friend of the Pereses since Binny could remember. And lately he had been with Binny's father day and night. As soon as Ian Khatib answered the door, Raanan pushed the newspaper in his face.

"Binyamin has seen this man," he said, and he poked at finger at Abdel Aziz.

"What?" Ian Khatib sputtered.

"Yes, this man! Do you know who he is?" Raanan Peres said.

"Here? In Kfar Darom?"

"Yes, maybe," Raanan said excitedly.

"Come in, come in." Ian Khatib backed up, waving father and son in. "This is terrible!"

"No, I don't know if I saw him . . ." Binny said helplessly. He could see where this was going. Before long, his father would have everyone on high alert because a known Palestinian terrorist had been in the streets of Kfar Darom. "It was in the paper. I think I saw him in the paper," Binny insisted. How could he tell them he had seen Abdel Aziz in person?

"His name is Abdel Aziz," Ian Khatib said, after putting on a pair of glasses and carefully examining the picture.

"Then you do know of him?"

"I do. And so do you, Raanan. He is one of Mawlawi Azduk's right-hand men. Very dangerous. Very self-righteous. Believes that only through death will his people be liberated. Death means nothing to this man."

Binny felt sick. How could this be Ahmy's father? One thing he was sure of was that he had seen Mr. Aziz standing with Mawlawi Azduk.

"Do you think the boy would recognize this man from the paper? From such a grainy photo?" Ian Khatib was asking Raanan Peres, completely ignoring Binny.

"I don't think we can take any chances. He is always out and about in the streets. He may have seen Aziz without realizing who he was." Raanan turned to his son. "Think, boy. Where did you see this man?"

Binny stood shaking his head.

"No, you misunderstood me. I was only asking about him because . . . I just . . . I have been studying people and names and . . . I thought I had seen him before, but I must have been wrong."

But they were no longer listening to him.

"This is it. We have been waiting for

something. We knew it was coming. I am sure that Azduk is behind this. He and his men are planning something soon. I can feel it."

"We must act quickly then," chimed in Raanan Peres.

"It is them or us," agreed Ian Khatib. Then, "You have done well, Binyamin."

With that, Raanan Peres beamed. It was the first time in a long time he looked proud of his son. Binny managed to nod his head and then looked at the floor. This was not going as he had planned. He had always hoped to make his father understand that peaceful talks were the only way Palestinians and Israelis could sort out their differences. Now he had brought a new battle to his father.

"Contact the men," Ian Khatib said to Raanan Peres. "We will assemble this evening."

7

AN EYE FOR AN EYE

HE hadn't been fully asleep. Somewhere, he could hear the occasional thud of a missile hitting a wall and the crackle of sporadic gunfire. Initially, the sounds were part of his dreams. But the sounds were getting closer, and Ahmy was beginning to rouse when a sudden bang jolted him. He sat straight up in bed, his heart racing. Before his eyes would focus, he heard his mother screaming. Ahmy scrambled from his pallet, still on his hands and knees, when he heard his mother cry out again.

Thunderous, terrifying noises filled their small home. In the dark, Ahmy could see green lasers flashing back and forth against the walls, floors, and ceiling. Israeli soldiers!

"No!" Ahmy's mother was screaming. She held Summi tight against her chest. Summi was also crying.

"Hiba!" called out Abdel Aziz. "It is okay. Please go back . . ." Ahmy's father was trying to tell his wife to be still, but she would not listen.

Ahmy heard a rustling behind him and turned to find Madi sitting up, rubbing his eyes.

"What is it?" he asked. His voice sounded so tiny, and Ahmy felt a sudden panic. He knew what was happening, but he couldn't let his little brother know. Israeli soldiers were doing a house-to-house search. At least, this was what they called it. It was really another terrorist tactic by the Israelis to frighten the Palestinians. After breaking down their doors, the soldiers searched their homes for any signs of resistance. They used heavy equipment to break through walls and plow through entire apartments.

Ahmy could hear the heavy footsteps of combat boots on the floor, tromping through their home.

He turned abruptly to his little brother and shoved him backward under a pile of blankets.

"Madi, you go back!" Ahmy whispered in a sharp tone. He could see that Madi's eyes were huge with concern. "Go back, I said. Under the covers," he said, pushing Madi back against the wall. He threw a pillow over the pile, trying to make it look like—

The small wooden door to their room was kicked open, and light from the living area flooded Ahmy's tiny room. Ahmy was still on the floor. He froze, peering up at two very large, very scary-looking Israeli soldiers. They were in riot gear, from head to toe—bulletproof vests, helmets, night-vision glasses, and assault weapons.

It was the sound of his mother crying that shook Ahmy from his frozen position. The first soldier pointed his gun at Ahmy. His mother tried to intervene but was pushed harshly to the side. Ahmy started to his feet.

"Mother!"

"Stay there!" commanded the soldier.

"Do as they say, son! Do not move," came Abdel's voice from around the corner. Ahmy could not see his father but found the sound of his voice suddenly comforting.

"What is that? Who is there?" the soldier pointed to the pile of blankets and pillows where Madi hid. Ahmy swallowed. His heart was in his throat. He prayed that Madi would not move. Any sudden movements might make the trigger-happy Israeli fire upon his little brother.

"Nothing," Ahmy insisted, although his tone of urgency gave him away. "It is nothing. Just blankets!"

The soldier stepped forward and kicked at the pile. Madi cried out, and the soldier jumped back, pointing his rifle. Panic filled Ahmy's heart.

"No! No!" Ahmy yelled, throwing himself over the pile of blankets. "He is my little brother. He is just a little boy. Do not hurt him. Please! He is just a little boy!"

"Come out," demanded the soldier, ignoring Ahmy's pleas. It was only when Ahmy instructed his little brother to come out that the soldier seemed satisfied. Ahmy rubbed his hand against Madi's back.

"You see," Ahmy said, trying to calm himself more than anyone else, "he is just a boy. A little boy."

"How old are you?" The soldier looked back to Ahmy.

"I am—"

"Noooo!" cried Hiba again. Summi's cries were escalating, and Ahmy could see the look of irritation on the soldier.

"I am nearly 14," offered Ahmy, trying to redirect the soldier's attention. He didn't want anyone getting mad at his little sister or mother. He was breathing more heavily. Ahmy knew what was happening. This was a part of the newest attack the Israelis had launched against the Palestinians—taking men and boys between the ages of 15 and 45. Israeli authorities had ordered the men and boys to turn themselves in for questioning about their possible involvement with Hamas, the Palestinian resistance group. But the men of Khan Yunis knew better than to do so. For that reason, the Israeli soldiers simply came in and took them at gunpoint in the middle of night. They took anyone they chose, and there was nothing the Palestinians could do about it. Perhaps they could fight back later, but there in the middle of the night, before their families and dressed in their night clothing, they had to cooperate with the soldiers.

Ahmy realized that this explained the raid tonight. They were taking his father away. They were taking Abdel Aziz away for questioning.

The soldier stared at Ahmy a moment longer, trying to decide about his age. Although Ahmy was lean, he was tall for his age. He could see that the soldier was trying to decide if he was lying.

"Stay where you are," he said finally. Ahmy let out his breath. He was unsure how long they had stared at each other. Behind the large soldier, Ahmy could hear his mother let out a loud sigh.

Ahmy would not see his father again that night. He could only hear more scuffling, the sounds of heavy boots and threats from Israeli soldiers. Ahmy could not hear his father's voice. Abdel Aziz was being very quiet. Mu'tasen Ajouri was another matter. He was the man who lived across the hall from Ahmy's apartment. He was a man said to be directly connected with Mawlawi Azduk, and he had a great temper. His voice thundered through the apartment building, echoing up and down the halls. He promised to retaliate. He promised to make each and every man present pay for their crimes against the Palestinian people.

As Mu'tasen Ajouri loudly struggled against the soldiers, Ahmy slipped out of his room and passed his mother who tried desperately to stop him. But Ahmy wanted to see his father before he disappeared. He wanted to see the soldiers who led the Palestinian men away. But by the time he got to the door, Abdel Aziz had been led out of sight. Ahmy lived on the third floor of their apartment building. The elevator had been broken for years, so he knew to look to the stairwell. Three men, including Mu'tasen Ajouri, were on the landing between floors two and three. Mu'tasen Ajouri had been slammed against the wall, pinned by two soldiers, but he refused to be quiet.

"You terrorize us, kill us, hound us . . . and you want me to cooperate?" Mu'tasen Ajouri practically laughed, but Ahmy could see that he was very angry. A man like Mu'tasen Ajouri never got scared by an arrest, just angry.

"We?" one soldier laughed back at Mu'tasen Ajouri and then to his partners. Everyone was laughing, but no one was having a good time. "We terrorize you? What about you and your people? You blow up our women and children, young and old. You don't care about anything. Life means nothing to you—"

"We live in fear because of you, and we only want Israelis to taste the same thing and lose their beloveds as we do!" Mu'tasen Ajouri shouted back.

"You are cowards!" the soldier shouted, shoving him even harder against the wall.

"You are killing us, so we kill you!"

"You sneak into our homes, blow up our cafés, buses, innocent people . . ." the soldier went on. Tensions were rising in the stairwell. Ahmy couldn't take his eyes away from the men. The voices practically shook the building, and Ahmy could feel more and more people creeping to their doorways to hear what was being said.

"You are killing us!" Mu'tasen Ajouri shot back. "What are we to do? Nothing? Sit back and simply let you take away everything that is precious to us?"

"Listen to him." The soldier projected a loud, fake laugh. "He acts as though he is the victim." Then the soldier turned back to Mu'tasen Ajouri and gave him a look so filled with hatred and menace that Ahmy shrank back a little behind the door, not wanting the soldier to see him watching them. "Let me tell you something. I just buried my brother. I just buried my brother and the girl who was going to be my sister-in-law. A beautiful, sweet girl. You know what she was doing when one of your suicide bombers came in and blew everyone up? She was sitting with a cup of coffee, talking to her friends about her wedding and dreaming of a future.

"And you people sit in your homes and think of ways to kill us. You are cowards. You cannot face us with your fight. You have to be deceptive. You are all cowards, and I despise you . . ." The soldier stepped back and moved as though he was going to use his weapon, but another soldier stepped forward, stopping him. None of this seemed to frighten Mu'tasen

Ajouri. In fact, it seemed to calm him down. Suddenly, he was very cool. His voice was quiet and even.

"Do you really think I enjoy this? We never had suffering like this before, not even during the '67 or '73 wars. I am against the idea of suicide attacks, 100 percent against it, but my people are desperate. You attack us with missiles from tanks and ships, by air and by sea. Many of us feel we have nothing to lose, so we are prepared for military attacks."

Ahmy poked his head out a little farther, wanting to see the expressions on the soldiers' faces. Mu'tasen Ajouri's voice was infectious. Everyone seemed to be mesmerized. No one was holding Mu'tasen Ajouri against the wall. He shook his head as he spoke.

"You have helicopters, tanks, and cannons. All we have are human bombs. It is the same, no? They all still take away our children and our hopes."

No one said a word. The soldier who said he had just buried his brother and future sister-in-law seemed to lose interest in Mu'tasen Ajouri. He made a small snorting noise then turned to go down the stairs. One of the other soldiers gave Mu'tasen Ajouri a small nudge, but everyone seemed to be calm.

Ahmy walked back into the apartment. It was true. It didn't matter what weapons were being used or how. Both sides were losing.

Sleep was impossible for the rest of the night while Ahmy waited for his father to return. Walking outside was impossible with Israeli tanks rolling around Khan Yunis. Instead, Ahmy sat on a ledge outside the kitchen door. Once upon a time, a balcony had been attached to the kitchen. A blast had blown off the balconies from one side of the building, leaving bits of metal sticking out. Ahmy's father had forbidden Ahmy from going out there, but he wasn't there to stop Ahmy tonight. While his mother tended to Summi and Madi, Ahmy tiptoed through the kitchen, pried the door open, and stepped out onto the narrow rods of metal. Carefully, Ahmy slid his back against the side of the building, squatting down on the beam.

The sun was just coming up, and there was a slight breeze—perfect weather. By all accounts, it looked like it would be a beautiful day outside. Except for the fact that his father was missing, in the hands of Israeli soldiers. Ahmy leaned back, letting his legs fall on either side of the beam. It was amazing how beautiful this land was when everything was peaceful. But the scene, he knew, was misleading. Sure, everything was quiet now, but many of the men from Khan Yunis were missing, being interrogated. Ahmy thought again about what Mu'tasen Ajouri had said. No one wanted war. No one wanted suicide bombers, but there seemed to be no other choice. They couldn't just sit back and watch everything be taken from them. Their political leaders could not be rounded up like cattle every time the Israelis felt like it. It was not right. Not fair. Not just.

"But you are wrong," came a voice. Although he was not yelling, it was strained. Whoever was talking was trying *desperately* not to yell. "It is not me! Whoever you think—"

"Shut up!" came another voice.

Ahmy leaned forward, holding on to the metal. Below, he could see a growing mob moving along the back alley. The men were back! He felt his heart leap and started to get to his feet, wanting to call to his mother and let her know Abdel Aziz would be coming home. He recognized many of the men as neighbors and shopkeepers. He saw Abdul's older brother Abassan and several of his friends.

Ahmy began to smile, but then he saw Mu'tasen Ajouri. He had been taken the same time Ahmy's father had, and Ahmy assumed that they were released at the same time. Ahmy opened his mouth to call out but stopped.

The men were not celebrating.

"I swear to you," cried out a man in the middle of the group. Ahmy bent at the waist, pressing the side of his face against the metal beam, and squinted down at the group. It was Mustasem Musa, a vendor at a clothing stand outside the main mosque in Khan Yunis. Ahmy knew him because his mother had bought clothing from him for Ahmy and his father.

"Traitor!" someone hissed, and Ahmy snapped his mouth shut.

"But it was not me," Mustasem Musa insisted. He was met with a hard shove from the back and almost fell over. Ahmy frowned.

"You will die for your deeds," someone else said. Low mutterings came from the crowd.

"No, it can't be," Ahmy said to himself.

"You were heard talking to them. Do you deny this?" another asked, and Mustasem Musa nodded his head.

"Yes, I do. I said nothing. I would not betray my own people to those . . . those animals. I would never!"

"Khader Abu Abbarra says different. He heard what you said. He heard you collaborating with Israeli agents, giving them vital information about Hamas and what we are trying to do," someone said. Mustasem Musa looked confused and pale.

"You are a traitor to the resistance and your people!"

"But it was not me! Khader Abu Abbarra is mistaken. He has mistaken me for someone else. He has made a mistake," Mustasem Musa insisted.

Ahmy sat speechless as the entire procession of men and teenage boys passed beneath him. For a moment, he forgot what they were saying and scanned the crowd for his father. Nothing. He could only watch helplessly as they led the accused Mustasem Musa away. Ahmy knew what was going to happen. There had been a growing movement of vigilantes in Khan Yunis and other refugee camps. Their goal was to stop Palestinian citizens from talking to Israeli officials at any costs.

The Israelis knew that the Palestinians had few resources left. It was said that they promised money and goods to people to report on the resistance movement so that the soldiers would know who to search for weapons. Ahmy knew that Mr. Musa would be hanged. Suddenly, he felt sick.

He started to swing one leg over the beam and stand to go back into the kitchen when he saw something else. He stopped, looked down, and saw Abdul. The two boys stared at each other for a moment. The reality of what he saw hit Ahmy. If Abdul told everyone that Ahmy had befriended an Israeli boy, he could have been hanged as a traitor. Worse, people might have suspected Abdel Aziz was involved.

"Abdul, wait!" Ahmy called out, making a motion with his hand for Abdul to stand still. "Wait!" But Abdul simply dropped his head and turned away.

Ahmy didn't wait. He whirled a leg around, losing balance for a moment, and had to dive toward the wall to regain it. He leaned into the building, turned the doorknob, and jumped back into the kitchen. His mother had just entered the room, and her mouth fell open when she saw where her son had been. Ahmy didn't stop. He flew past her, skidded around the corner, and ran out the front door. He took two and three steps at a time, running down the staircase. He sped around the corner of the building and almost ran right over Abdul, who was standing on the side, waiting for him.

"Oh. Uh, sorry. I . . . wanted to talk to you . . . about . . ." Ahmy struggled to catch his breath. Abdul wasn't interested.

"What are you?" came Abdul's voice.

"What?" Ahmy was caught off guard. "What am I?"

"What are you?" Abdul repeated.

"I don't understand." Ahmy furrowed his brows at Abdul. *What was he talking about?*

"Are you Abdel Aziz's son? A freedom fighter with the resistance? Or are you a friend to the Israelis? To that kid from Kfar Darom? Are you sympathetic to their beliefs? Or are you a Palestinian?"

Ahmy shrugged his shoulders, rubbing his eyes for a moment. "Come on, Abdul. You know what I am."

"No, I don't." Abdul's tone was flat. "Mohammed was killed, and you brought that . . . kid to the funeral. What was that, Ahmet? A show? Our schools are hit by missiles, our fathers are dragged into the street for questioning, our mothers weep, and you do nothing."

"You know where my heart lies," Ahmy said, but Abdul shook his head.

"Before Mohammed was killed, I would say 'yes.' Today, I am not so sure. So . . . I have to ask."

"What do you want me to do?" Ahmy asked, and Abdul smiled.

AN EYE FOR AN EYE

IT had not taken long for word to travel that Palestinian terrorists had been lurking within the walls of Kfar Darom; and it was suspected that one Abdel Aziz, a reputed right-hand man to Mawlawi Azduk, was involved.

Binny groaned and drove his small spade into the soil, turning it over and over. How had things spiraled so far out of control? Not just within the last few days, but in life, in the history of humankind and religion? He admitted he didn't know that much about other religions and countries, but he was sure the world wasn't supposed to be like this!

He turned more soil and unconsciously poked a finger into the rich, cool mound. It was perfect soil for potting. But he wasn't thinking about farming or gardening. He was thinking about Ahmet Aziz. Ahmy didn't seem like someone who could be the son of a known terrorist. Ahmy seemed to be like Binny. He wanted to know about other worlds and cultures. He wanted to know why things had gotten so bad, and he hoped he could figure out how to change them, how to make them better. Maybe that was why he had liked Ahmy from the moment he saw him. Binny could sense that Ahmy was out of place. He didn't fit with his father, just as Binny was mismatched with Raanan Peres.

In recent weeks, the violence had escalated to new heights in the Gaza Strip and West Bank. But there had also been a shift in the world's reaction. For decades, the world had sympathized with the Israelis because of Hitler, because of the PLO and its horrific terrorist attacks. But now the world was seeing the Israelis as the bad guys. Binny smiled grimly over this. Bad guys? What did that mean? The two sides were trying to destroy each other in the name of all that was holy. Who was bad, and who was good? The Israelis had a powerful army. The Palestinians had nothing. So they resorted to terror. For now, it seemed, the world saw only that the Palestinians were helpless. World leaders were calling for a ceasefire and the implementation of the Saudi Plan. Some even accused the Israeli government of provoking the Palestinians so that the level of violence would get so bad it would be impossible to put the Saudi Plan into action. At the same time, a new militant antipeace movement was growing within the Israeli community. A small but very powerful group of men vowed that they would bring far more destruction and violence before they gave up one hectare of Israeli-occupied land. And, in recent days, it became clear to Binny that his own father was part of that group.

How could he be the son of someone so opposed to peace? Worse, his father was committed to violence as a "solution."

It made him sick. It made him think of something he had read before, some biblical reference. Binny poked at the dirt a while longer, wondering where he had read what he had read, trying to remember exactly what it was.

"The son and the father," he muttered to himself, trying to extract the exact words. Nothing came.

A noise.

Binny turned his head, looking up at the wall. Instinctively, it was the first place he turned to for a strange noise. There had been too much activity at the wall of late. Strangely, he wasn't frightened. Briefly, he was a little excited. He hoped to see Ahmy's face peek over the wall. He dropped his spade and was about to stand when he heard a voice. No, many voices. Binny shrank back a little. He could only catch phrases here and there, but it became clear what was happening. Young Palestinian men had discovered a way into Kfar Darom. Binny's mind raced, wondering if Ahmy had told other people. Had Ahmy betrayed him? Or had it been Abdul?

Binny wanted to run. He wanted to turn and head down the alley into the main street, loudly warning everyone that Palestinian terrorists were coming. Binny was no fool. He knew what destruction a determined group of Palestinians could bring upon his people. But he could not move. For some bizarre reason, he stayed where he was. He needed to see if Ahmy was among them. Actually, he needed to know that Ahmy was *not* there. But something tingled in the back of his head, making his brain buzz with recognition. So when Binny did see Ahmy's face peering over the wall, quietly instructing others how to enter, where to jump and land, Binny's heart sank. *It was him.*

Binny found himself flat against the far wall, folded in between the plant sunshades that were attached to the wall. They were the perfect camouflage.

Abdul landed first.

"It's clear," he said, looking back up at the wall. Binny recognized Abdul's older brother and his friend who had attacked Ahmy and Binny in Khan Yunis the day of the funeral. Binny had believed they hated Ahmy, so it was a terrible surprise to see Ahmy with them. Ahmy scanned the area quickly then turned to catch knapsacks thrown down into the garden.

"Sometimes guards do come here, so we must hurry," Ahmy offered, and Binny felt his chest tighten. He was no different from the others. He had befriended Binny simply to gain access to Kfar Darom. Binny's eyes narrowed as three more young men made their way over the wall, gathered their backpacks, and hurried toward the alley that led to the center of Kfar Darom. Binny held tight. Stepping out now would only get him killed. His only chance was to wait until the Palestinians were out in the open, near soldiers. At that point, Binny decided, he would give the alarm. His eyes shifted back to

Ahmy, who had stopped at Binny's tomato patch. Ahmy knelt down and plucked a ripened tomato from the vine and examined it.

Thief!

Then Ahmy noticed the small spade and picked it up. He looked around the garden for a moment as though he expected to see Binny.

"Are you coming?" came Abdul's voice. Binny could no longer see him, and he knew Abdul was at the mouth of the alley. A panic began to fill Binny's heart. *They were going in!*

Ahmy looked up and nodded, letting the tool drop to the ground. He was carefully packing the tomato in his sack when he saw Binny. At first, Ahmy only saw his feet, but Binny could see Ahmy's eyes slowly traveling up Binny's body, partially hidden in the mesh netting of the shade.

"Come on!" came Abdul's voice again.

Binny and Ahmy locked eyes for a moment, and neither moved. Then without a word, Ahmy nodded toward the alley and headed that way. Binny could feel cold sweat pouring down the sides of his face and back. He waited another ten seconds and then stepped out, following Ahmy's group.

It was as though Binny had a second person inside his head, yelling at him. *They are inside! They are inside!* Binny heard the words, saw Ahmy with his friends, and felt terror about the backpacks. Surely they held something terrible like homemade bombs or guns, but he just couldn't bring himself to believe Ahmy was there to harm him or his people. On the other hand, he knew about Abdul and his hatred of the Israelis. And he knew that the others had sworn revenge for the Palestinians who had been killed. He also knew that there had been another sweep just the day before by Israeli soldiers of Palestinian men and teenage boys.

Carefully, he stepped into the alley only to see Ahmy's back disappear into the crowd. Binny quickened his step. If the rumors were true about Abdel Aziz, then he had to realize that Ahmy could be just as dangerous. *Was he there to do a "job" for his father?*

As Binny exited the alley, he desperately scanned the crowds for any sign of Abdul or Ahmy. Had this day been three weeks earlier, it would have been much more difficult to see the boys. But more and more Israelis were staying at home, too frightened to venture outside for fear of the growing violence, especially the suicide bombings. Merchants and shoppers still filled the streets, but Binny could identify Ahmy easily enough. He was tall, wearing a blue shirt with English writing on it. A sports shoe company logo that was very popular made Ahmy look as Israeli as the next guy. Binny broke into a trot, trying to catch up to the group but being careful not to be seen.

Binny knew Ahmy had seen him. Wouldn't Ahmy know he'd follow their group, Binny wondered. But Ahmy never looked around. He looked straight ahead, as though he knew exactly where he was going. In fact, they all did. It was an eerie sight. In all, there were five Palestinians in Kfar Darom, and they looked as comfortable as they could be. They must have a specific target in mind, Binny thought.

Anxiously, Binny weaved through the small crowds, making sure he did not bring attention to himself. He scolded himself the entire time. He should be yelling out, "They are here! Terrorists! Look, see them!" He should be yelling his head off, making sure every man, woman, and child knew who they were and what they were up to. The trouble was, he didn't know. Before he set a crowd upon them, he needed to understand what was happening. Maybe . . .

It was ridiculous. Why else would Abdul and his no-good brother and friends be here except to take revenge for Mohammed's death? Binny could think of no other reason. They passed clothing, food, and shoe stores. They passed a small video and appliance store and a newspaper vendor. They passed a café, and they appeared to be headed straight to the main entrance of Kfar Darom. For a moment, Binny entertained the idea that they had simply broken into the settlement just to see if they could. After all, wasn't that what Ahmy had done the first time they met? Binny could feel a wave of relief washing over him. Then, as suddenly as it came, it was gone. The group stopped at the crossroads between the entrance and Main Street. Abdul's brother was doing all the talking.

Yell now! Now!

Binny watched helplessly as they split up. Ahmy and one from the group went in one direction toward the police station while Abdul, his brother, and another friend appeared to double back. Binny ducked behind a parked car, his heart suddenly pounding. If Abdul saw Binny, it would all be over. Whatever weapons or explosives they might have, he would detonate on the spot.

Binny squatted down, peering under the car between the wheels. He could see the feet of Abdul and his friends coming and rolled around to the other side of the car so as not to be seen. The voice inside his head raged on. He had to do something! Now it was apparent that something was going to happen. Something awful, something dreadful, something deadly.

He hoped to hear what Abdul was saying to tip him off to their plans, but the trio was completely silent.

"I cannot just sit here," Binny gasped. He half stood, still hiding behind the car, and watched Abdul, his brother, and his friend disappear. Then taking a deep breath, he dashed across the street, running parallel to Abdul and his accomplices but careful never to pass them. As he darted and weaved among shoppers, he glanced over across the street.

Twice he nearly bowled someone over. He was petrified that Abdul would look over and recognize him.

Suddenly, Abdul stopped. Binny tried to stop so abruptly that his shoes skidded sideways. He reached out and grabbed a store doorjamb to stop himself. He was breathing heavily, and his head was pounding. The voice inside him was screaming at him to sound the alarm, to finger the Palestinians before they did any harm. Everything seemed to be happening in slow motion and fast-forward at the same time. Binny felt utterly helpless and confused. Although his brain was moving at warp speed, everything had become painfully slow. Abdul was talking to his buddies now, slowly taking the pack off his shoulders and swinging it around in front to open it. Binny stepped into the middle of the sidewalk, reaching out with his hand. This was it! Abdul talked on, so nonchalant. He unzipped the bag while he spoke, nodding his head. One of the others, Abdul's brother, looked around as they talked, and Binny sank down again.

A paper. Or a map. Abdul pulled some kind of paper from his pack, and they studied it for a moment. All three crowded around the paper, looking it over. Binny's eyes darted left and right. Didn't anyone else notice them? Wasn't anyone suspicious? But no one seemed to notice the three school-age boys. They looked like anyone else. They were dressed like most boys Binny's age. They looked like three guys who were talking about some kind of note or piece of paper. What was so wrong about that?

Then Abdul pointed farther down the road. Binny looked too. What was there? His mind raced, trying to remember what was down that way. More stores. A café. The school. So many possibilities. They were off again, and Binny darted back across the street, this time hanging closer behind them. He was running out of time. He knew it.

Instead of following the boys, Binny ran through an alley and headed toward his apartment building. The voice in his head was winning. He knew he had to do something.

He ran faster than he ever had. He never knew he could run so fast. Although his heart pounded painfully and he wanted nothing more than to stop, his legs would not. They pumped harder and harder, carrying him to his apartment building, up three flights of stairs and directly to Ian Khatib's home. Binny pounded on the door so hard he could hear his voice and fists echoing up and down the stairwell.

"Coming," Ian Khatib said irritably, although Binny suspected he was somewhat startled by the urgency of Binny's pounding. When he saw Binny, he really looked surprised.

"Binyamin?"

"I . . . have no time to explain." Binny was nearly doubled over in pain. He wheezed so hard it was difficult to make himself understood. He waved his arms for a moment. "They are here," he said over and over again while Ian Khatib tried to figure out what he was talking about.

"Who . . . ?"

"And they are carrying something . . . They are here, and they are going to do something. Café maybe. School. I don't know. They are here . . ."

"Binyamin, you must slow down. I can't understand you. Where is your father?" Ian Khatib was trying to calm Binny down, but there was no time. Finally, Binny grabbed his hand. For a moment, Ian Khatib pulled back. But the expression on Binny's face told him to follow. Binny tried to get Ian Khatib to run, but he wouldn't.

"Do not ask me how I know. I can tell you all that later," Binny said. "But there are terrorists here in Kfar Darom. I saw them come over the wall of the garden. They have backpacks, young, my age. They hate us. They are here, walking the streets right now, headed toward the west end."

Finally! He was able to get it all out. Ian Khatib did not question him as Binny had been afraid he would. Instead, he muttered something under his breath, turned, and ran back into his apartment. For a moment, Binny stood still, trying desperately to catch his breath. He could hear Ian Khatib yelling into a phone. But it was nothing compared to the pounding Binny had in his own head. *Ahmy, Ahmy, Ahmy*. Binny had told Ian Khatib about Abdul, his brother, and his friend, but what of Ahmy and his buddy? Where were they? He couldn't bring himself to say anything about Ahmy. *Ahmy, Ahmy, Ahmy!*

Binny turned and ran back down the stairs, leaping over sets of steps and landing hard. His feet pounded. He could hear Ian

Khatib calling after him, but there was no time to stop. He had to go back to find Ahmy, to stop him from whatever he thought he was going to do.

"Binyamin!" Ian Khatib's voice echoed down after him. "Where are they? What do they look like? Binyamin?!"

No time. There was no time, and Binny didn't know how he was going to make it all the way back through main street toward the entrance gate. To where? The police station? Binny threw open the door to the apartment building and headed toward the settlement entrance. Ahmy could be anywhere now. Anywhere!

Ahmy

THE PALESTINIAN PLAN

IT was a different world, this Kfar Darom. Ahmy looked around. There were clothing and food stores everywhere, no doubt run by prosperous merchants. The stores looked plush, clean, and expensive. It was hard to understand why the Israelis would want Khan Yunis, where most of the men were jobless, children were shoeless, open sewage ditches paralleled the littered streets. Yet the Israelis were killing people in an attempt to get that land. Ahmy was disgusted. And the bitter irony that his own father had once been a successful merchant on this very land had not escaped Ahmy. The plush stores he was looking at could have easily been his own.

Since the night the soldiers took his father, Ahmy had watched huge changes occur. It was funny because he really hadn't thought things could get worse. But they had. He heard—he could not watch—that Mustasem Musa had been killed by other

Palestinians. More tanks rumbled into Khan Yunis, wreaking havoc such as Ahmy had never seen before. Suddenly, the streets were empty as most residents huddled in their homes. Even that did not ensure their safety. The Israelis seemed to be randomly shooting through walls, demolishing homes. Ahmy eventually heard that these were the homes of suspected militant leaders. Mawlawi Azduk's home had been destroyed, and Mr. Azduk disappeared. Ahmy was afraid because his father had been connected with Mawlawi Azduk. Tanks and foot soldiers were all over the place. Israeli snipers were posted on rooftops, occasionally picking off people who were suspicious. Unfortunately, under their rules, every Arab was suspicious. While Binny sat in his pleasant little garden, Ahmy and his friends were being picked off by bullets.

In Kfar Darom, things were quite nice. But in Khan Yunis, the scars of war were everywhere. Half buildings stood, their interior exposed where a shell or missile had hit. It was so strange. Some rooms were completely destroyed, while other rooms looked as though the walls had simply been removed. In other places, metal doors were blown to pieces, and walls were riddled with bullet holes. On the main road, a car had been completely flattened by a passing tank. The Israelis didn't care what lay in their path.

After each attack, the Palestinians were always back in the streets as soon as it was safe. They worked together to clean up things. They wanted all signs of Israeli terror gone, but it was useless. Wreckage, broken glass, and buckled streets were everywhere. The attacks did more than simple material damage to buildings and businesses. Most men did not work anyway. Most families were already so poor there could be no real concern about property damage. The true problem was what was happening to the Palestinians as a people.

Maybe it wouldn't have been so bad had Ahmy never known a better life. But he had. His memories as a child were sketchy, but he did have some. He could remember his mother laughing. He could remember his little brother, and he could remember what it was like to own something. He'd had things. Nothing that really mattered to him now. Maybe a truck, a book, or an extra pair of shoes. But they were his. Yet every time the Palestinians were forced from their own homes and made to run like criminals, they lost pieces of their lives—pictures, heirlooms. Now they were turning on one another. The violence was escalating. They were losing pieces of themselves. Ahmy knew that his father was not a violent man. He was a loving father and husband. But times had changed Abdel Aziz and so many others. The situation in the Middle East was not getting better; it was only getting worse.

Abdul had asked Ahmy what he was. It was a good question that started Ahmy thinking. At first, he really couldn't say. He had no home. He had no future. He had nothing. He could only listen to Abdul while he searched for the answer.

"I do not know about you," Abdul had said, "but I intend to find my home again one day. My real home. The place where I was born. Where my family comes from. God willing, one day I will find my home." And Ahmy understood. As long as he did nothing, he *had* nothing.

He scribbled a note to his mother, asking that she not cry for him. Whatever was to become of him, he wanted her to be proud and to know that her son was fighting for what should have been hers. A house. A home. A place where Madi and Summi could grow and prosper. As he wrote the note, he thought of the place his father had once described to him. It was a place where he once stood, the closest he could come to an earthly-based paradise. Ahmy asked Adham Daoud, a small boy born with just one leg, to carry the note to his mother. Adham tucked the note into his pants pocket and scurried off on crutches given to him by the United Nations. But they had been given to him long ago, and the crutches were too small, so Adham had to lean over, making him look very disabled. It was a ruse he used on the Israeli soldiers. In truth, Adham could scale just about any fence, wall, or building. He was small, but he was powerful. He was also trustworthy. Ahmy knew he could depend on Adham to deliver the message to his mother. It was the last time Ahmy allowed himself to think of Madi, Summi, or his parents.

Ahmy knew as long as the Saudi Plan was ignored, nothing would change. In fact, things would get worse. The Israelis were increasingly taking more land in the Gaza and

West Bank territories. Although the Palestinians were ready to acknowledge Israel as a true state, the Israelis were not ready to give back the land they took. Land they stole! So the resistance fighters had come up with a new plan. Ahmy knew his father was part of the plan as well. They would no longer sit back and wait to be attacked. Always when the Israeli tanks rolled into Khan Yunis, there was terror and surprise. With the attack on Mawlawi Azduk's home and family, he had come up missing. Some said he was in hiding; others claimed that the Israelis had him. No one knew. But with Mawlawi Azduk missing, a new man stepped in. Bahjat Abu Skheila swore that he knew of Mawlawi Azduk's whereabouts, that he was safe and plotting revenge against the Israelis. He made promises of victory! Maybe some people liked the sound of victory, and others liked to hear that Mawlawi Azduk was alive and well. Whatever it was, the men of Khan Yunis greeted Bahjat Abu Skheila warmly.

"We can fight them with our bare hands, with stones. We do not need to have the weapons they have. Even with a stone, I can defend Jerusalem and Palestine," Skheila cried. "The Palestinian people will never give up a single grain of its soil."

The response had been silence. There were no cheers. A quiet, powerful rage swelled up within the crowd, and Ahmy could feel himself becoming overwhelmed.

"Hey, you cowards!" Bahjat Abu Skheila turned toward Kfar Darom. "We swear we'll answer your aggression. Just wait." His voice was deadly intense. Then he turned back to his listeners and made a promise to them. When the Israelis returned to Khan Yunis, "We will be waiting."

Word spread quickly that Israeli soldiers were approaching Khan Yunis through the narrow alleyways and barren streets. Only this time, hundreds of the camp's young militants were waiting. Armed with weapons taken from fallen Israeli soldiers or rocks and slingshots, the young men hid behind buildings and abandoned cars while a small, carefully selected group of militants fled on foot toward the walls of Kfar Darom. When Abdul's brother Abassan told Bahjat Abu Skheila that his little brother and Ahmet Aziz had been inside the walls of Kfar Darom, they were chosen to lead a raid party.

This time, Ahmy did not think about Binny, the Israeli boy. He thought only of the land of paradise his father spoke of—the land his family deserved. He thought about the question that Abdul had asked him. He knew what he was. He was Palestinian. He was proud and angry. Very, very angry.

But when he had made it over the wall of Kfar Darom and saw the garden, it was difficult to push the image of Binny from his mind. He had been a good friend. If only for one afternoon. When Ahmy stopped to pick a tomato, he thought of how generous Binny had been, giving his enemy tomatoes to take back to his mother. But Ahmy had not allowed himself to think further of Binny. He was on a mission for his people. It was as Bahjat Abu Skheila, Mawlawi Azduk, and his father had all said. Defying the Israelis, even if he died, was the cause. Not one single grain of their soil would be given to the Israelis without a fight!

Abdel Aziz had his own paradise in mind. With a dreamer's smile, he had described the world where he wanted to raise his family. It was a simple house made of mud bricks with a wooden door, no lock and no need for one. It was in a small village, miles from where they were in Khan Yunis. It was open, bountiful, and set in a golden wheatfield, shaded by fig trees and grape arbors. It was so perfect, so majestic, so wonderful, storybooklike, and so seemingly improbable that Ahmy couldn't shake the image from his mind. He could see it. He could smell it. He could taste the figs and grapes and feel the wheat in his hands. A mud-brick house. Was it so much to ask?

The sight of Binny had choked Ahmy with fear for a moment. Not that he was afraid of Binny. Binny was no fighter. And it wasn't that he was afraid Binny would warn the settlers. Actually, he didn't care. It was a strange moment in which Ahmy felt mostly sorrowful. But he couldn't speak. He could not explain something to Binny that Binny would never understand. Binny was destined to see the world through his little garden. Binny couldn't know what it was like to live in the conditions that were normal for Ahmy and other Palestinians, to know how depressed his people were, and to realize that there was no future for his little brother and sister. He couldn't tell Binny he was sorry for what he was about to do because he wasn't. He didn't want anyone to get hurt, but resistance was vital. Because of Israeli aggression, everyone *was* getting hurt!

Ahmy stood staring at Binny for a second, wishing he could explain all this to him, but he could see in Binny's eyes that he would never understand. Binny's eyes narrowed, and Ahmy knew Binny thought he had been betrayed. He wanted to tell Binny that it was not true, that this had nothing to do with him. But there was no time. The plan was in effect. Even as he stood there, he could hear the clanking, heavy treads of tanks gouging tracks into the crumbling streets of Khan Yunis. The noise reminded him that he must move.

What are you? What are you?

Ahmy watched Binny's eyes narrow, calling Ahmy a liar.

"Ahmy!" Abdul's voice called to him.

What are you? What are you?

Ahmy turned and entered a world he had never seen before, making his father's simple house seem so much more reasonable and deserved. He saw smiling faces. Young women, their heads uncovered, laughed and joked with one another. Ahmy scanned the crowds. There were also people who looked concerned, even frightened. But still it was a completely different atmosphere. There were people shopping. The children had shoes. Business seemed to be in order.

Ahmy kept his head down and followed the others until they reached a street corner. It was agreed they would split up. Abdul, Abassan, and Salihbin Saud would go to the schools. The plan had been one that Ahmy liked. So much propaganda had been given to the Western world about the Jews, particularly because of the way they had been treated by the Nazis. But the world didn't seem to know or simply ignored the fact that the Israelis were doing the same thing to the Palestinians. When their tanks came rolling through the refugee camps, destroying everything in their paths and frightening children and threatening adults, the West was silent. No one said a word when the soldiers shackled and questioned boys and men for hours and hours. And no one seemed to care that the Israeli government marked the

Palestinians with ink, numbering them like cattle. It was just what the Nazis had done to the Jews in the concentration camps.

The Israeli peace movement was demanding peace talks. So the resistance fighters had agreed they should attack the Israelis from the inside—starting with their children—but without violence. The plan was to place hundreds of leaflets in the schools. And the irony was perfect. They were the same leaflets dropped on the Palestinians by the Israelis, only their words of lies were blackened on one side. The truth was told on the other.

Ahmy turned left, moving up the street with Raminah Abayat toward the entrance gate. But as he did, he saw Binny. Binny was shadowing them, hanging close enough to watch what they were doing but hoping not to be seen. Ahmy frowned. He was sorry it had to be this way, but Binny would have to accept what they were doing. It was the only way to bring about peace. Generation after generation was fighting. They had to break the chain. If each new generation was educated and understood, they would refuse to fight. And when Ahmy allowed himself to think this way, the mud-brick house in a golden wheatfield did not seem so impossible.

He watched Binny over his shoulder for a moment and then continued on with Rami, who spoke in low tones.

"We will have justice soon, my brother," he was saying. Ahmy nodded.

He took a few more steps, thinking about the tone of Rami's voice. Suddenly, he turned to his partner.

"But this is a mission of peace," Ahmy said, suddenly needing confirmation from Rami. "We are the new resistance fighters with a new method of weapons, yes?"

Rami snorted. "This should be one state, and the Israelis are welcome to live here . . . under our rules," Rami said.

Ahmy groaned internally. "They will have their own state. It is the compromise we are seeking." Ahmy worked to keep his tone low, not wanting to bring any attention to himself or Rami.

"Even if we reach a compromise, there will be a reaction by the military from different factions."

"What is this about factions?" Ahmy asked, disgusted. This was typical of Rami. Ahmy was equally disgusted with himself. He should have known better about Rami. He was a hothead, like Abdul. He would never want to use peaceful means if he could fight.

"For every group that agrees to peace, three more groups will pop up and fight against us," Rami explained, sounding annoyed that Ahmy would not know such things.

"But that is what we are fighting against," Ahmy countered. "Listen, I don't like the Israelis any more than you. But killing isn't working." Ahmy dropped his voice as he and Rami passed in front of the entrance gate, which was heavily guarded by Israeli soldiers.

"I don't accept that," Rami said when they had passed the gate. Only a few yards away was the police headquarters.

Don't accept . . . *what?* Ahmy wondered. He had a dreadful, sinking feeling in his stomach. He had no great love for the Israelis. He really didn't. He wished every day and every night that they would fall off the face of the earth. But they were here, and they were powerful and capable of doing even greater damage than they already had. But somewhere in the back of his mind, it had occurred to Ahmy that there could be a hundred more Binnys in the Jewish settlements. It wasn't the *people* he hated. It was the Israeli government and its policies.

"We're not here to hurt them, are we?" Ahmy asked.

Now he knew what Binny had felt. Ahmy had been a fool. He had been led to believe they would throw two homemade bombs. The first was to be a dud. It would cause panic, making everyone inside the building run out. They didn't want a body count, Ahmy had been led to believe. They wanted to destroy the buildings. They wanted to bring down the buildings that sheltered the police and their weapons, just as the Israelis had done to Palestinian buildings. It was a good plan. It was also a huge risk. If they were caught, they would be shot immediately. But Ahmy had been told they would begin destroying structures not people, buildings not families.

"The first one is to be a dud," Ahmy reaffirmed. Rami said nothing.

"We don't want to have anything to do

with this kind of fighting," Ahmy said, his voice getting louder. They were getting closer to the headquarters. "It is possible, you know, that Palestinians and Israelis could live side by side. It is possible!"

Ahmy had entered Kfar Darom angry. He was there for a purpose. He was ready to die for his people and the cause, but killing Israeli policemen wasn't the cause he was fighting for.

"But the Koran doesn't say that," Rami shot back, and Ahmy stopped dead in his tracks. His mouth fell open for a moment.

"What do you know about the Koran?" Ahmy sneered. "I don't think I have ever seen you study this—"

"Why are you being so loud? So stupid? What do you care about these Jews? Or is it as Abdul said? Did you make friends with a Jew boy? Are you crazy? They don't want peace! Look what they have done to us. Even the prophet encourages us to kill Jews!" Suddenly, they were face-to-face. Both were so angry, they had temporarily forgotten who was around them or how loud their voices had become.

"No, he did not say that! Again, you are taking things out of context to fill your own desires of hatred and anger. This is not what he said. This is not what the Koran teaches. You are—"

A huge explosion from the other side of Kfar Darom rocked the earth. Everything shook, and Ahmy nearly lost his balance. A bomb. It must be. He gasped, jerking his head over toward the other side of town and then back to Rami. Rami swore under his breath.

"We are late," he said and began hurrying toward the police headquarters.

Only moments ago, Ahmy had been thinking how different the worlds between Kfar Darom and Khan Yunis were. Yet at that moment, they were identical. He could hear women screaming, children crying, and sirens starting to howl. A moment of peace was suddenly replaced by terror and confusion. Ahmy saw that Rami was breaking into a run toward the police headquarters.

What are you? What are you?

Abdul's voice rang in his head.

Abdul! Ahmy knew that it had been Abdul who detonated the bomb. Ahmy squeezed his eyes shut for a moment. His friend was gone. He knew it. He could sense it. The message of peace was gone.

What are you? What are you?

Rami was in a full run toward the police station. No one thought anything of a young boy running to the police. He was just like everyone else—afraid.

"No!" Ahmy yelled after Rami. Then he was running himself. It was to be the chase of his life.

Binny

THE ISRAELI PLAN

BINNY burst out of the apartment living quarters and headed south on the main street toward the entrance gate. It was the last place he had seen Ahmy and the other Palestinian boy. It was a funny thing, but Binny wasn't afraid. He did not fear Ahmy or his actions in any way, and yet Ahmy was a virtual stranger. Still, he had felt something intrinsically good in Ahmy. Ahmy cared about people. Not just his own but all people. He, too, was tired of all the violence and misery. But this . . . Binny had never expected that Ahmy would come into Kfar Darom with foot soldiers. Were it anyone else, Binny would be sure of suicide bombings. Still, he hoped otherwise.

He had just turned right, headed for the entrance, when the blast from behind pitched him forward. His right hand jutted out, scraping along the pavement and catching him from falling flat on his face. He staggered but regained his stride.

Still running, he looked behind him and licked his lips. *What was that?* But he knew. Abdul! It had to have been Abdul and the others. But where? The school? He winced. How could this be? How could they do this? How could Ahmy be a part of this? How could Ahmy have looked right at him in the garden, his garden, even taken some of his tomatoes, and then moved on, like it was just another day? How could Ahmy be part of something so awful?

Binny's feet struggled to keep up with his mind as it raced at an alarming rate. Everything Binny had ever read, saw, heard, and felt about the Arab/Israeli conflict whizzed through his brain. He wasn't stupid. He knew what the Israelis were doing with their tanks and machine guns and random checkpoint searches. He knew that thousands upon thousands of Palestinian civilians had been displaced from their homes. He knew all that. And he knew what the rest of the world was saying about the Israeli tactics. Bullies, they were called, and worse. Not so very long ago, the same sort of things were being said of the Palestinians. The Muslim world was known for its terrorist acts. The world knew this. In the United States, on September 11, the whole world saw firsthand how vicious Muslim rage could be. But suddenly, everyone was turning on the Israelis because they had more sophisticated equipment than the Muslims. That was the difference! Nothing else.

The only other argument was that the Israelis were taking land from the Palestinians. But who took the land from whom? The answer depended on how far back one wanted to go in history. Most Muslims chose only to go back seven centuries. But the land truly belonged to the Israelis. If a person really wanted to get technical, the land had always belonged to the Jews. At least, this is what Binny had read in the Old Testament.

But Binny didn't want to get technical. He saw it this way: He was here, and Ahmy was here. His people, Ahmy's people. No one was going anywhere, and blowing each other up wasn't working. For so long, Binny had tried to understand the hurt and anger of the Palestinians. To the consternation of his own father, Binny had sided with the Palestinians at the dinner table, debating with his father. He wanted his father to see the other side of the argument. But the truth was, Binny knew the real problem—Muslims needed to take an honest look at their rage and then redefine who they were and how they wanted to live.

As Binny was running down the street, he could hear people screaming. Somewhere he could hear a woman calling to her child, and he slowed his pace a bit, looking left and right. The name sounded vaguely familiar. Then he saw a woman kneeling, arms open wide, and a small child climb out from under a car. The woman was crying. The grief and relief on her face said everything about how everyone was feeling. Disbelief, shock, anger, fear. How much longer could this go on? How much longer would the Muslims, or specifically, the Palestinians, be willing to sacrifice their young to get something they were never going to get?

The wailing of sirens flooded the air. Binny's head began to throb from the noise. People were running frantically for cover, while others called out the names of loved ones, loudly praying that they were still alive.

Most, it seemed, ran toward the sounds of the explosion, making it more difficult for Binny to move against the crowd.

Everything Binny's father had ever said about the Palestinians was coming true. They disregarded the sanctity of life. In Kfar Darom, the young were expected to attend school, read, learn, and embrace life with the idea of one day contributing to their community. But in Khan Yunis, just steps away from Binny's world, the Palestinian youth celebrated suicide bombings against the Jews as their source of dignity.

Now Binny could see the entrance gate. Soldiers were on full alert, and they had shut down the gate, letting no one in or out of the settlement. Two or three were using walkie-talkies, trying to get more information about the explosion, where and how it had happened. As Binny drew nearer, his eyes scanned the crowd. There was no sign of Ahmy, so he cut to the left as he approached the soldiers. They barely gave him a second glance. They had seen his face before. He was just another scared civilian looking for a loved one.

He hated to run. He had never been a runner. But his legs were pumping faster than ever. He could feel his heart pounding, and there was a slight level of pain in his chest. He ignored it. He had to. He didn't know how much time he had before he could find and stop Ahmy.

Exactly what he was planning to say to Ahmy, Binny wasn't sure. He had to look at his face, see his expression. Again, Binny just could not believe that Ahmy was ready to die so young, so easily, so needlessly. Ahmy had taken a tomato from his garden. Binny remembered that as he ran along, fists pumping, eyes constantly scanning. He had taken fruit. Would a boy who was about to blow himself up do such a thing? Binny's mind flipped back to a memory of one of Ahmy's friends. He had stolen tomatoes to give to Mohammed's family as a symbolic gesture of taking back from the Israelis. Was that why Ahmy had taken the tomatoes? Binny felt a sudden surge of panic. He had lulled himself into believing that Ahmy wasn't capable of doing something as horrible as blowing up a building or innocent people. But the tomatoes . . .

Ahmy!

Not far ahead of him, Binny spied the back of Ahmy. He, too, was running. He was running toward the police headquarters. Binny wanted to yell, he tried to yell, but his voice choked. He was so winded, he had nothing left. His legs had gone into autopilot. It was ironic that when he was ready to yell, he had no voice. He could not yell, but he could still run. He focused on the back of Ahmy.

Ahmy and his partner were running toward the building. They were going to blow up the building!

There *were* other options! Binny wished he could scream that at the top of his lungs, say it on the radio, or write the letters in the sky for all the world to see. There were other options. The Palestinians could say, "We will oppose the Israelis, but we will oppose with nonviolent resistance! We will build schools and our society and our economy. We will create jobs and build hope." But instead, they thought of and spoke of and acted only in violence.

There were other options. That thought pounded in Binny's head as he charged after Ahmy. As they got closer to the building and he could hear the sirens and screams in the background, an anger began to build in Binny. He wanted nothing more than to catch Ahmy and put his fists against him, but he was too far away. Ahmy and his partner would reach the building before he could stop them.

Ahmy stole his tomatoes, lied to him, tricked him into thinking he was different. He used Binny to gain access to the garden and . . .

Binny slowed instinctively for a moment. His eyes grew wide for a second, not sure he was actually seeing what was happening before him. Ahmy had made a huge lunge toward his partner, who was only a few steps ahead of him. Ahmy landed hard against the other boy, dragging him down. They seemed to fall in slow motion. The other boy was fighting back against Ahmy, trying unsuccessfully to continue his run. He could not hold up the weight of Ahmy and fell to the ground. But he managed to roll over, pinning Ahmy below him.

"What are you doing?" he snarled at Ahmy. Binny could hear every word as he came upon them. His shadow fell over the boy, distracting him long enough for him to look away from Ahmy. Ahmy made a wild swing, connecting with his friend's jaw. Moments later, Ahmy was on top.

"You lied!" he barked back at the other boy. Binny stood back, confused.

"You weren't ever going to throw a dummy! You knew . . ." Ahmy was saying, but his friend was not listening.

"Get off of me, you fool!"

Ahmy held on.

"Traitor!" the boy yelled. His arms were flailing, trying to use his thumbs against Ahmy's eyes. Ahmy struggled against him, whipping his face from side to side but refusing to release his hold on the boy. At last, the boy felt his backpack. His left hand pulled it close, fumbling to open it. Ahmy saw it and yelled at Binny without ever looking at him.

"Grab it! The bag! The bag! Get the—" Ahmy commanded Binny. Binny pounced forward and snatched the bag from the other boy.

"Jew lover!" the boy hissed at Ahmy then spat in his face. "You will pay for this! You will die as Mustasem Musa did. A traitor. A pathetic—" he started to say, but Ahmy cut him off.

"Shut up. You lied. You are the traitor. What about the peaceful resistance? What is that to you? Do you really think we can go on killing and dying like this?" Ahmy's words were strained as he struggled to hold the other boy down.

"I don't care what you think, you coward. You are no Palestinian. Abdul protected you. Abdul died for his people, for the cause. He is a hero. But you . . ." the boy sneered.

Like an old crocodile, the Palestinian boy emitted a deep, low growl. There was a sudden burst of energy, and Ahmy seemed to fly off him. The boy rolled over and leaped to his feet. Ahmy skidded backward in the dirt. Before anyone could react, the kid was on Binny, punching him in the face and grabbing the backpack from his hands. Binny staggered to the right, almost falling, but he stayed on his feet. He, too, felt a sudden raw power he never knew he had. He spun around and charged after the boy who was making a second run at the police station.

"Get him!" Ahmy yelled in Arabic. His voice seemed unusually loud. There was a panic in his voice, and several soldiers from the entrance gate looked over. Binny didn't wait. He was fast on the heels of the boy who only made three easy steps before Binny made a diving tackle. Just as Ahmy had, Binny dragged the kid down. He wrapped him up tight, locking his arms around the boy's waist. Binny made up his mind that only an explosion would blast his hands apart.

"Get him!" Ahmy was yelling again, jumping to his feet and coming to Binny's aid.

Ahmy hit so hard, he practically shoved Binny off of the kid. He made an "oof" sound as the two collided. Binny fell to the side, still fighting for the bag.

"Get the pack. Get it out of here," Ahmy was saying. Binny and the kid seesawed back and forth with the bag until, at last, Binny wrestled it free. Ahmy had helped, pounding on the kid's arm with his fist, making him lose his grip on the handles. The kid unleashed a fury of curse words and appeared to be getting a second wind. He was about to get the upper hand on Ahmy when three soldiers descended upon them. One large man shoved Ahmy aside and grabbed the Palestinian kid by his shirt collar. The kid was like a paper doll in the man's hands.

"What is going on here?" asked the second solider. He was angry. Of all times for the boys to engage in an after-school fight . . . But his expression changed quickly upon hearing the words of his comrade.

"This kid is Palestinian!" the voice boomed, and Binny cringed. The man holding Ahmy's friend was staring down at the kid, his eyes turning coal black. Immediately, Binny could understand why the Israeli soldiers had such a fearsome reputation. Binny was looking at one of the most frightening, angry-looking men he had ever seen.

The other man, nearest to Binny, looked back and forth between the boys. He focused on Binny. Binny's eyebrows shot up as he feigned innocence.

"Not me!" Binny exclaimed, throwing his hands up in the air. The man nodded.

"I know you. I know your father." He nodded. His gazed shifted toward Ahmy, while the other kid continued to struggle against the soldier. He was too stupid to stay quiet and began hurling insults and threats against the soldier in Arabic.

"We will get justice!" he squirmed.

"Shut up!" the first solider snapped. He looked as though he wanted to kill the boy but managed to control himself.

"You cannot stop us and until you—"

"Shut up!"

The second soldier looked back at Binny.

"You were trying to stop him," he said. It was more of a statement than a question. Binny nodded, still huffing to catch his breath. "What is this?" he asked, pointing to the backpack. Binny shot a look of uncertainty at Ahmy.

"Who are you?"

"A traitor!" hollered the boy. "A Jew lover! You should love him," he laughed without a trace of humor in his voice. He looked crazed with fear and anger.

"You are a Palestinian," the second soldier said accusingly to Ahmy.

"But he was helping. Don't you see . . . he was trying to stop the bombing!" Binny stepped forward, but the third soldier was on top of Ahmy before Ahmy could do or say a thing. He jerked Ahmy off his feet, grabbing his shirt and slamming him down to the ground.

"Help? To help kill us? Set off more bombs?"

"No, no. He stopped this one. Didn't you see? He tackled him, stopped it from happening." Binny was waving his arms frantically. It was true. He had been right all along about Ahmy. Whatever the reason that

Ahmy had initially come to Kfar Darom, Binny no longer cared. What mattered was that Ahmy had stopped another bombing from happening. This caught the soldiers off guard because they had seen Ahmy and Binny fighting together against the other Palestinian boy.

"Why?" the soldier asked in Arabic. "What are you?"

Binny watched as Ahmy turned into a statue. He simply stared back at the soldier as though he hadn't understood the question or didn't know how to answer.

"Why?" the soldier demanded again. Binny could see more civilians and soldiers making their way over to their gathering, and he cringed. The people of Kfar Darom were angry and tired of being attacked. Binny knew that a mob would quickly form and grow violent if they knew they had two bombers in their hands. "Why? Why are you here then? What are you?"

Was he a friend of the state? A friend of Israel? This was what the soldier wanted to know, but Ahmy just stared at him. He said nothing. More and more people were coming.

"He is a fellow human being," Binny piped up.

The soldier's eyes narrowed. He maintained his firm grip on Ahmy's shirt. Behind him, several men ran toward them, two holding cameras, and Binny's heart pounded. Journalists. They only made things worse. Because people saw the press as their way to send a message, people on both sides screamed and ranted and raved to the press, making threats and promising revenge. Binny could see that the mob was ready to form. Once, Ahmy had stepped in front of Binny to protect him, but Binny wasn't sure he would be able to protect Ahmy now.

THE BOTTOM LINE

IT was true. He was panicked about what was going to happen. Ahmy was no fool. He had seen how the Israeli soldiers treated his people. Binny was standing next to him with big eyes, looking so innocent. He didn't know Israeli soldiers the way Ahmy did. As soon as they discovered he was Palestinian, he was as good as dead. Ahmy knew this. And if they didn't kill him and Rami, Rami would see to it that he was killed when they returned to Khan Yunis. Ahmy had prevented a suicide bomber from completing his mission and achieving his entrance to paradise. Ahmy's family would be shamed, possibly stoned. There was no winning here. And yet, Ahmy was satisfied with what he had done. He had been led to believe that this was a peaceful resistance action. It was something he believed the Palestinians should have been doing all along. But when the soldier threw him down to the ground and he saw the look on his face, Ahmy knew nothing had changed. He had stopped Rami from bombing the police headquarters, and for a tiny moment he felt he had done something good and made a positive change for the world. The look on the soldier's face proved otherwise. He didn't see a look of gratitude but one of hatred.

Abdul was gone.

Abdul had lied to Ahmy, knowing he would not go along with any other plan. But Abdul had probably really believed he was doing Ahmy a favor. Oddly, he had probably thought he was saving Ahmy's soul.

For a moment, staring back into the eyes of the soldier who hated him so much, Ahmy wondered whether his life was worth saving. The violence and hatred was never going to end.

He had chased Rami down, tackled him, and fought him for the backpack. It really was a miracle that the bomb had not detonated during all the tugging back and forth. He had fought against his own countryman. Then out of nowhere, Binny had appeared and fought with him to get the bomb from Rami. At the time, Ahmy had been glad for Binny's help, but now Ahmy could see things for what they were. He had fought side by side with his enemy. He was a traitor. Ahmet Aziz was a traitor. How could he ever return home?

Two soldiers dragged Rami off, kicking, screaming, and shouting obscenities to Ahmy.

"This is not over," he yelled at Ahmy, his legs kicking wildly at anything he might be able to hit and hurt. "You are dead! Do you hear me? You are dead, disgraced. Your family is disgraced—" But his voice was soon drowned out by a chorus of shouts back at him from more and more civilians who had gathered around to see what was happening.

But nothing brought that realization faster to Ahmy than when the solider asked him what he was. It seemed to Ahmy he had heard that question a lot. What was he? Friend of Israel? A Palestinian? A freedom fighter? A resistance fighter? A coward? A traitor? Son of Abdel Aziz?

What was he?

It was suddenly quiet with Rami gone.

For the first time, Ahmy faced Binny. He could have said thank you or blamed him for his new troubles. Instead, he simply asked, "What am I?" He pressed his hands out, shrugging his shoulders. Under the blistering heat, standing in the middle of the settlement and surrounded by Israelis and angry soldiers, he could only laugh. What else could he do? His life was over. He couldn't go home, and he could not stay here. There was a certain bitter irony about the fact that his life was over because he had *saved* a Jewish settlement. But he hadn't done it for the Jews. He would want his father to know that.

"What do you mean?" Binny kind of laughed back at him.

"How can I . . . ?" He couldn't finish the sentence. He was surrounded by people who would never understand. Ahmy could only shake his head. His life was over.

Ahmy could never go home again.

"You did the right thing," said Binny. "What are you? You are right. Justified. You are a hero." Suddenly there was an echo of his sentiment around them, and Ahmy looked around to see many people nodding their heads, proud of this stranger—a Palestinian. Word had traveled quickly that a Palestinian boy had stopped a second attack. He was being heralded a hero—something Ahmy wanted no part of.

"But it changes nothing," he said. "You will not stop. Your tanks will not stop. Even now."

He waved a hand to the far-off distance. "You can hear them tearing through Khan Yunis."

"We do this because your people are killing us," a voice said from the crowd. "We do it to protect ourselves."

"Protect yourselves?" Ahmy shook his head. "Your tanks against our flesh?"

"But it is your flesh that has been killing us, sneaking into our settlement and killing our children," another woman spoke up. "One of your friends blew up a schoolhouse today. Does this seem right to you?"

"No," Ahmy said flatly. A strange silence fell over everyone for a moment. Then a camera was pushing forward. A journalist wanted to talk to the Israeli and Palestinian boys who had taken down a bomber. Ahmy frowned. But he did not pull away. What was done was done. He could not know what his future held, but he would speak out for his father.

"The tanks and midnight searches are just a continuation of the Israelis targeting Palestinians," said Ahmy.

"But there are killers living near you," Binny said gently. "Our soldiers search for weapons from your men who kill."

"Says who? Your soldiers? Your soldiers who shoot without provocation?" Ahmy forced an insincere smile.

"Do you believe that these men, the resistance fighters, are innocent?" Binny asked back.

"You kill us because we kill you because you kill us because we kill you . . ." Ahmy said, staring down at the ground.

"But the killing began because you are trying to reclaim land that was lost to you," came a voice from the crowd. The tone was calm, relatively quiet, but Ahmy could hear the edge in that voice and others. They would believe only what they believed. The same was true of his own people. Ahmy said nothing.

"The Palestinians would kill us for this land because we have shopping and crops," said a thin old man, stepping out from the crowd. He was different from the others. He didn't feel like being nice to the Palestinian hero. He scowled at Ahmy. "You would kill us for all this?" He spread his arms out. Others joined in, and Ahmy could feel the mood of the crowd shifting. The old man was beginning to whip up the settlers again. Ahmy poked his chin in the direction of Khan Yunis, a refugee town with knee-high trash, with broken sidewalks and crumbling buildings.

"And you would kill us for even less."

A hiss came from the crowd. Then, "Binyamin!" a voice cried out, and a trim, clean-cut man pushed his way through the crowd until he reached Binny. At first, relief washed over his face. He turned his face up toward the sky, murmuring some kind of prayer. He grabbed Binny and hugged him. Then he turned on Ahmy.

"This is him?" he bellowed, not waiting for an answer, and he lunged at Ahmy, wrapping his fingers around Ahmy's throat. "You little thug! Have you nothing better to do with your life than bring misery and death to others?!" Binny was tugging furiously at his father.

"No! Father! This is Ahmy! He helped us. He stopped the boy who was going to blow up the police station. He helped us, Father!"

Raanan Peres loosened his grip a little. He looked more confused than anything else.

"You know his name."

"Yes, Father. I know him. I knew him from before today. I know him, and he is good, Father." Binny was practically shouting.

"You know him!" Mr. Peres repeated in disbelief.

Everything that Mr. Peres said, Ahmy could imagine, would be the way his own father would react. Abdel Aziz would be just as angry and dismayed to learn his son had befriended a Jewish boy.

"How do you know him?" Mr. Peres demanded.

Ahmy had been staring at the ground, but he looked up at Binny for a moment, and the two exchanged glances. Ahmy would say nothing. Nothing mattered anyway. Instead, he would let Binny say whatever he wanted. He would not blame Binny for anything he might say.

But Binny told the truth, and a small gasp echoed around the crowd.

"From the garden. I have shared tomatoes with him."

"Then," came a deep voice, "this must be yours." Everyone looked over to see a soldier who had discovered and searched Ahmy's backpack to find a plump tomato. In the scuffle, Ahmy had completely forgotten about his pack. He nodded. Oddly, in the midst of everything that was happening, he was happy to see that the tomato was not damaged.

"They blow up our buildings, our buses, our streets. They try to destroy us, and now they are taking our food!" shouted the old man, turning his back on Ahmy, facing the crowd. He raised his hands in anger. "Is there no end to what they will do? What they will take?"

It was Binny's turn now, and Ahmy knew exactly what he was feeling. He could see the look of hopelessness on Binny's face. What would happen when the cameras went away and Ahmy was gone? He would be known as the kid who had befriended a Palestinian boy. He shared tomatoes from his garden—the settlement's garden—with the enemy. Everything Ahmy was thinking and feeling, Binny was experiencing too.

It was impossible for Ahmy to know *why* he liked Binny. Maybe it had been the way Binny tended his garden. He had always looked peaceful. Maybe it was the same way Ahmy would look if he owned a mud house in a golden wheatfield surrounded by fig trees. Or maybe he liked Binny because he looked as if he might know something about the kind of peace that Ahmy wanted a part of. Now Ahmy was seeing Binny doing one of the bravest things he had ever seen. He had been wrong about Binny. He had said Binny wasn't a fighter. But he was. Maybe not with his fists but with his words. And he proved to be a much stronger opponent than anyone was prepared to deal with. At least, on that day.

"He took only as much as I gave him. And he was thankful," Binny said, reaching forward to take the backpack out of the hands of the soldier. The soldier did not protest, and Binny handed the backpack over to Ahmy. Tentatively, Ahmy took it. Binny smiled. "I wanted to give him more, but I wasn't sure about him. You know, I have heard so much about the Palestinians, I was ready to believe the worst. But I learned a lot about him and his people.

"I disobeyed you, Father. I went over the wall and attended the funeral of a small boy in Khan Yunis."

Raanan Peres staggered backward.

"They cry like we do, grieve like we do. And they cry for revenge, just as we do. I heard them, and while I was there, I understood their grief. He was, the boy, I mean, a good boy. He didn't deserve to die. Just like our own. But it keeps happening. It is what my friend Ahmy says. We kill because they kill because we kill because they kill."

"Binyamin! You must—"

"I must speak. Shouldn't we put a stop to this? Shouldn't we do everything we can to make the killing stop? I have heard that the Saudi Plan is being pushed by the Westerners, but we don't like it because we don't want to give up land we now own. Muslim radicals don't want to call Israel a legitimate state. Maybe the Saudi Plan is not for us, but who would ever know? We are all too busy counting bodies to do anything else, and I am tired of it."

His voice rose higher and higher.

Raanan Peres had gone pale, and Ahmy could see him looking sideways, trying to judge what other settlers were thinking. Binny might have seen it too, but it didn't stop him. He would speak his mind without interruption.

"Is it so bad that I should make friends with one we call the enemy? Is it not better that I should teach him about us and learn from him rather than we kill each other? Is it not better that I share a tomato than a bullet or a bomb?"

No one said a word.

Ahmy knew there would be those who did not agree with Binny. There were people from his own camp who believed Israeli occupation was so evil that the only way to resist it was with bombs and bullets. For them, as long as there was an Israeli presence, there would never be peace. Ahmy knew this because his father was one of those believers. Abdel Aziz would never see Binyamin Peres for who he really was. He would never understand how his own son could like an Israeli boy. And the fact that Ahmy brought home and fed his family two of Binny's tomatoes—it was a betrayal Abdel Aziz would not soon forget. But would he ever forgive? Ahmy felt so conflicted. He knew what was right, but he loved his father very much. Part of him felt he should punch Binny in the face, just for the show of it. But he couldn't. He never could. Binny was a good guy.

Raanan Peres struggled to keep his voice calm. "You do not know what you are saying, son. He is not your friend. He is your enemy." There was a round of mumbling, and Ahmy could feel people staring hard at him. "Why did he come here today, Binny? Ask yourself this? Why did he come here?" Binny opened his mouth to protest, but his father held up his hand. "Today he changed his mind." He looked over at Ahmy and shook his head. "For whatever reason, today he changed his mind. But what about tomorrow or the next day? He may not change his mind."

Binny looked from his father back to Ahmy. Ahmy said nothing. What could he say? Ahmy started to shake his head but stopped. Binny had no reason to trust him. He had come to scare the Israelis. He had wanted to be part of a resistance movement for his people. He had chosen peaceful protest, but now there was no reason anyone should believe him. As long as Ahmy could remember, as long as the history between the Israelis and Palestinians, there had never been trust. Why should it start today?

A deep sadness swept over Ahmy. He looked into the angry faces of all the adults who surrounded them. Men, women, soldiers . . .

"But," Binny said, "today he did change his mind." He looked back at Ahmy and stuck out his hand. "Today, my friend, I trust you."

Ahmy could hear the shutter of a photographer's camera clicking madly, taking pictures of the boys shaking hands. He could hear the rumblings of disbelief around them, and still, the sounds of war all around as well. Ambulance sirens wailed, and in the far-off distance, tanks rumbled through Khan Yunis. But they were all tiny, insignificant sounds compared to the one that filled his heart. "My friend." And he felt his heart leap—just a little.

Maybe today, the world would change—just a little.

"What am I?" Ahmy asked Binny.

"What do you mean?" Binny asked back. And he told Ahmy that he was a hero. He had done the right thing. He tried to tell his friend that he should be proud of his actions, but Ahmy would not accept it. He shook his head.

"But it changes nothing," Ahmy said. "You will not stop. Your tanks will not stop. Even now, you can hear them tearing through Khan Yunis." His voice was accusatory and angry.

Binny was taken aback. His mouth fell open for a moment, as he tried to think of what to say. Binny turned his head for a moment, trying to listen. But he could only hear the sirens. *What was Ahmy thinking?*

A bomb had just exploded in the settlement, killing who knew how many people.

Someone spoke for Binny.

"We do this because you are killing us," a voice said from the crowd. Binny looked to see who it was. Not everyone spoke Arabic. Binny looked to see Tzipi Shemes staring back at Ahmy.

"Protect yourselves? Your tanks against our flesh?" Ahmy said, his voice getting louder. Binny wanted to jump on him, to shut him up. This wasn't the boy he had met at the wall. But the crowd didn't know about that boy. Ahmy was arguing back against the crowd that grew by the moment. Binny's heart fell. He was no longer listening to the words of the crowd and Ahmy. He could see his father coming toward him. And he wasn't going to wait for any formal introductions. He would attack the boy, call him names, and demand for justice to be done. Justice that would include imprisonment for Ahmy—and he would be lucky if that was all he got.

They were all the same, the Israelis and Palestinians. Binny understood now that Ahmy knew this too. It was why he had stopped the attack. It was why he refused to go along with more deaths. Binny didn't even have to know the exact reasons that had brought Ahmy to Kfar Darom. Wasn't it obvious? He was tired of sitting back, having nothing to claim for his own, having no control over his own life. At least for a while, Binny had had his garden. Perhaps to others this would seem silly or insignificant. But to him, it added purpose to his life and provided something for his family. It had meaning. Maybe Ahmy just wanted a taste of Binny's life. It was true that Binny was better educated. He could speak three languages. Binny had been allowed to study comparative religions so that he could better understand the different views of Jews, Muslims, and Christians. He had ample books and luxuries Ahmy could not imagine. Ahmy came from a world where his people hated and distrusted their neighbors. He came from a world where they were held prisoner inside the walls of their homes and feared the anger of their Jewish neighbors. Both boys had fathers who would die before making friends with their neighbors. And both saw little future other than hatred and violence. Both boys were sick of it.

And both Binny and Ahmy were about to be found out by neighbors, family, and friends. Each had befriended the enemy.

Binny's mind raced as he looked at his father accusing Ahmy of things he had not done. It was something he had read and tried to figure out. "No one who denies the Son has the Father. Whoever confesses the Son has the Father also." *Where had he read that?* He had been studying so many different religions . . . He thought about its meaning. But there were so many. How would Ahmy return to his father, and how would Binny tell his father that he knew this Palestinian boy?

But he did. And so much more.

Mr. Peres had asked how Binny knew Ahmy in Hebrew, but Binny answered in Arabic. He wanted Ahmy to know what was being said. He had met Ahmy in the garden, had shared tomatoes and even the experience of attending a Palestinian funeral. Raanan Peres was furious. Binny knew that he had hurt his father deeply, but he wanted his father and everyone else to understand that the Palestinians were so much like the Israelis.

No one who denies the Son has the Father.
No one who denies the son has the father.

Binny could see his father's face turn purple. He saw the finger pointing at Ahmy, the yelling to the crowd. Raanan Peres was a man who believed the Palestinians were his natural-born enemies, and they could never be friends to Israelis or their nation. Never! He was no different than Abdel Aziz. It was just as Ahmy had said. *We kill because they kill because we kill because they kill . . .* It didn't matter how it had started. It was time for it to stop. But he couldn't deny what the Palestinians were doing. Maybe it was worse in Khan Yunis, as Ahmy had told him. He didn't know. He wasn't there every day. But he was in Kfar Darom, and he knew that the suicide bombers in the main streets had to stop. It was just . . . insanity.

Whoever confesses the Son has the Father also.

Whoever acknowledges the son has a father also.

Binny knew his father loved him. He knew this. And from what Ahmy had said, he was sure that his father loved him also. Maybe it was enough. Maybe it wasn't. He didn't know. But his father had taught him to read, to love the written word, and to explore new thoughts. Raanan Peres, the teacher, not the anti-Arab, had always said he wanted so much for his family. He bought books and taught Binny how to tend his garden and to believe in things that couldn't always be easily explained.

Binny put an arm around Ahmy and publicly called him "friend." He could not imagine how his father would react, so he looked only at Ahmy. Binny heard several people in the crowd draw in deep breaths.

❖　　❖　　❖　　❖

It was strange that everything Binny had been through and everything he felt about his experiences with Ahmy were neatly summed up in three simple sentences with the Associated Press, sandwiched between the newest reports of fighting between Israel and Palestine.

In the midst of another violent outbreak between Israelis and Palestinians, two boys managed to kindle the most unlikely of friendships. Binyamin Peres, an Israeli resident of the Kfar Darom settlement, met Ahmet Aziz in the neighboring Palestinian town Khan Yunis where the two slipped in and out of their two worlds, building such a strong friendship that Aziz would defy the growing suicide bomber movement to prevent more deaths in the Kfar Darom settlement. While Aziz was unable to stop the bombing of a schoolhouse, he was able to prevent Raminah Abayat from bombing the Israeli police headquarters.

It said nothing of how they had met or what had become of Ahmet Aziz since that fateful day. Binny poked at the ground a little, rearranging the tomato plants. So much had changed. So much was the same. Guards were posted permanently in the garden, and Binny's sanctuary was gone. He still came to the garden every day, but it was different. Although the guards never spoke, just knowing they were there changed things. Binny had always enjoyed being alone. Now, like it or not, he always had company.

Periodically, he looked up to the top of the wall, hoping to see Ahmy's face peering over at him. It was pointless, and Binny didn't know why he still looked. Razor-sharp barbed wire had been strung along the tops of the walls, making it more of a prison than ever. The other side of the wall that had once offered a crumbling brick structure of stairs had been sealed. Once, in a moment of frustration, Binny lobbed a tomato over the wall and listened to it land. He wanted to see if anyone called out on the other side. Even if it hit someone, Binny would have been happy to know someone was there. Maybe he could call out, send a message along to Ahmy, or inquire about him. Instead, he did nothing. No one responded to the tomato because no one could approach the wall.

Very methodically, Binny created a third row of tomatoes. New seeds that he had ordered from a catalog long ago—long before the bombing of the schoolhouse and the disappearance of Ahmy—had finally come in.

Already reconstruction was underway for a new school. A plaque had been erected for the three teachers and two students who lost their lives in the blast. It was business as usual for most merchants, and there was an ongoing debate between the Palestinians and Israelis about the land. Things had quieted down again, but everyone remained watchful. It was just the way of the world.

Binny had read about a cemetery in northeastern Africa, just outside the city of Asmara in the country of Eritrea, where Jewish, Muslim, and Christian soldiers were all buried together. The small country, across the Red Sea from Saudi Arabia and Yemen, had once been engaged in a bloody battle during World War II. It was funny that not so very long ago, these men could be buried alongside one another, but Binny and Ahmy could never live in the same manner.